TO HIDE FROM
DEATH

TO HIDE FROM
DEATH

Where do you go when death is lurking?

THERESA MORETIMER

authorHOUSE®

AuthorHouse™
1663 Liberty Drive
Bloomington, IN 47403
www.authorhouse.com
Phone: 1-800-839-8640

This is a work of fiction. Names, characters, businesses, places, events and incidents are either the products of the author's imagination or used in a fictitious manner. Any resemblance to actual persons, living or dead, or actual events is purely coincidental.

Published by AuthorHouse   03/25/2013

ISBN: 978-1-4817-2960-4 (sc)
ISBN: 978-1-4817-2958-1 (hc)
ISBN: 978-1-4817-2959-8 (e)

Library of Congress Control Number: 2013905020

ACKNOWLEDGEMENTS

I wish to thank Paula Anstine for the wonderful job she did modeling for the book cover for me. You did an outstanding job! I wish to thank Mark Anstine and Mark Anstine Photography. Mark, thank you for not only modeling, but the photography as well. I would not have a book cover or a portrait of myself if not for you! The friendship I have with you and Paula can never be replaced. I love you both.

I wish to thank Wes LeRoy and the entire AuthorHouse staff for the wonderful job they have done publishing my book and for their patience with me.

I wish to thank my beautiful daughters for putting up with me and my irritability while writing this book. Your words of encouragement kept me going.

Thank you Mom and Dad for always being there, and giving us a place to come home to when there was nowhere left to run. I love you both!

Shana, thank you for your constant encouragement. I couldn't have done this without you!

This is the day our Lord has made.
Let us rejoice and be glad in it

Psalm 118:24

The rain poured and the roads were flooding. Thunder drowned the screams coming from the little three bedroom cottage. If there were passersby, they would have never suspected the gruesome scene inside that little home. Kelly tried to talk her way out of the house but Eric had all the doors nailed shut with the exception of the kitchen door.

Tears were streaming down her thin face. Her eyes more piercing blue from the reddened whites. The bruises were already beginning to show. She was pleading with Eric to just let her go. She reached for the phone from the kitchen wall in desperate hopes of calling 911. As her trembling fingers punched the numbers on the keypad, he ripped the phone cord from the wall. "He's going to kill me and there's no one who can save me now" thought Kelly. "God, please let me get out of here alive," she silently prayed . . .

CHAPTER ONE

It was a beautiful spring day and Kelly finally had the nerve to go out. Her friends had asked her to go with them to the local bar and have a few drinks. She found this funny because that was code for we want to party and need a designated driver. She smiled to herself at the thought.

"You haven't been out since the break up between you and Eric. Don't you think you deserve a little down time?" She asked herself.

The phone was ringing and Kelly answered the one in the kitchen. "Hello" she spoke into the receiver. "Hi, it's me." Her heart skipped a beat at the sound of Eric's voice. "Hi, how are you?" she asked. Kelly couldn't help still having feelings for the man.

"I wanted to know if you could bring the kids over here Sunday and watch a movie, I thought maybe I could spend some time with them. I really miss them Kelly. I miss you too. I thought maybe you and I could talk."

"Talk about what?" She asked, tears threatening to fall.

"Us" he said. "I'm so sorry Kelly. I didn't mean to hurt you. I love you, and I love the kids. I'm going to classes now, it will never happen again."

Eric was saying everything she had wanted to hear. "Are you really?"

"Yes babe, I am. I haven't been drinking any liquor and only a few beers now and then. I haven't done any drugs either. I'm changing Kell. I'm changing for you, the kids and our marriage. I don't want to lose everything I have. You're my world."

The threatening tears followed through and began streaming down her face. Could this be real she thought to herself? Could he really change? "Ok, I will see you Sunday. What time should I bring them over?"

"How about one?" he asked.

"That's fine. Church will be over at noon and I can give them lunch first."

"How about I make them pizza like I used to?"

"Ok, we'll see you at one on Sunday."

Kelly's heart was pounding in her chest as she replaced the receiver with trembling hands. She never thought this day would happen especially after what she had done. Eric had considered it the ultimate betrayal, worse than if she had cheated on him. She wiped her tears from her cheeks with the backs of her hands. Her mind racing back several months ago, when she caught him getting high in the girls bedroom and took pictures of it.

"Why did I text those pictures to his daughter?" she asked herself out loud. That incident almost got her killed. She had never seen him angrier than that night. She shook her head.

She wanted to stop the flood of memories filling her mind. But the memories had other plans.

Her mind drifted back to when she first met the man that was now her husband. He looked so cute in his baseball cap and hunting clothes. He had a bottle of beer in his hand and kept calling her beautiful. She thought about when she had gone with him to look at Steve's house. Eric was staying there helping him with improvements.

Kelly should have known that night not to see him again. "How many men show you a house carrying a loaded .357 in their hand and using it to point to the work they had done?" she asked herself aloud. "You should have bolted for the door" she chided herself. He was cute and you were lonely she thought to herself. "Then he kissed you under the moonlit night and you fell under his spell" she said woefully. She didn't want to admit it, but she let the wrong part of herself rule that night.

She thought about the second month they were dating and how good he was at what he did. The man knew how to make a woman feel sexy and desirable and she had such low self-esteem. He definitely knew all the places to touch that turned a woman on.

"Easy now girl" she chided herself. "You know you can't trust him. Don't let your libido get in the way of thinking straight." She walked over to the coffee pot and poured herself a cup. She picked up the Irish Cream coffee creamer and added some to her coffee. "I wish you were the real thing today" she told the creamer half smiling.

Kelly picked up the phone to call her sister. She needed to walk and talk today, but there was no answer. "I guess I'm on my own" she said aloud. She picked her jacket up from

3

the counter and put it on. "Maybe I will go see my therapist instead" she said smiling and walked out the door toward the pasture.

"Apache" she called. The big, handsome paint came trotting to the gate where Kelly stood. Goldie the palomino Haflinger was already there. "Hello Goldie, I see you've been enjoying your hay" she told the horse. The mare nickered softly but when she realized there were no treats, she walked back to her hay pile.

Apache nickered and shook his head at Kelly. "Hello boy" she said. "How is my favorite guy today?" He nickered again softly as if to answer. Kelly stepped through the gate and headed toward the barn. Apache followed right behind her. Kelly picked up a brush and turned to her best friend and began brushing him. He shook his head up and down and pawed the ground. "I'm sorry big guy, I forgot."

Kelly went in the barn and came out with a tear of hay and dropped it at Apache's feet. The big gelding put his head down and began munching on the hay while Kelly brushed and began talking. She started brushing him in long easy strokes, speaking to him as if he were a person.

"Apache, Eric called and wants me to bring the girls over Sunday" she began. Apache picked his head up and turned his neck to look at her and whinny. "I know. I know," she began. "But he says he's changing. He says he's going to meetings and that he's not the same guy anymore." Apache pinned his ears back and stomped his big front hoof. "I know, I thought the same thing. But what if it's true this time Apache? What if he's really changing? I still love him in spite of everything."

Apache picked up his big head from eating and shook it. It was to get rid of a fly, but looked like "no, he isn't" in horse talk. He looked back at Kelly who was almost finished that side and ready to move to the other. She said "I know you don't like him Apache, you never have. But he's my husband and I have to try. I have to exhaust every effort to make this marriage work. I took a vow before God, in my church" her voice rising with the latter part.

Apache snorted. "I'll be careful Apache, the kids will be there. He's never hurt the kids" she said and Apache stamped his foot, and looked at her. Kelly crossed behind his big romp, patting him to let him know she was there. As she approached his neck, he rubbed her with his nose. She walked in front him and said "I love you Apache!" The big tri colored paint wrapped his neck around her then nudged her with his nose.

"I know you love me Apache" she said smiling, and hugged him again. She walked back to his side and began brushing. Apache stood there like a champ. He always did. He never had to be cross tied to be groomed because he just stood so well.

Kelly asked Apache what he thought she should do and he raised his head in the air and let out a big whinny. "You really don't like him boy" she said kissing him on his head. "I love you big guy. You will always be my husband horse. Now go out there with Goldie and enjoy your day. We'll go for a ride later when Aunt Brenda gets here.

Kelly put the brush back in the barn and rubbed Apache's head before he walked back to the field. "You do realize I'm going to do this right?" she called to him. He snorted and began to walk back to Goldie. Kelly smiled.

CHAPTER TWO

It was a nice night for early spring. A little on the chilly side but nothing a light jacket wouldn't handle. Kelly was heading out the door to drive her friends to the bar for a few hours. She needed to get out. She needed to clear her head. Tonight was not a night for being home and thinking. No, she needed to be with friends.

"Hey Kelly!" called Rita and Ryan from across the yard, "We are so glad that you came out tonight" they said in unison. "You need this as much as we do" Ryan told her, and they all laughed together and Kelly headed toward the local bar.

They walked inside and Ryan put some quarters on the pool table. "Which one of you girls want to play me?" he asked. "I will" said Rita. "Good, you rack and I'll break" he said winking. They were all laughing and Kelly laid a twenty on the bar and ordered two beers and a coke. She slid two dollars back to the bartender when she received her change and gave a beer to each of her friends.

The night was moving kind of slow she thought to herself. "Hey Kell" what are your plans for the weekend?" asked Ryan. "I have to take the girls to see Eric on Sunday" she winced as she said it.

"Are you out of your freakin' mind?" asked Ryan. "Did the dumbass bug bite you on the ass?" his voice had raised a little.

"No. But he wants to see the kids, and they want to see him. They don't know everything that happened, Ryan." Kelly said in a defensive tone.

"They know that he locked himself in their room to get high in their bathroom. Isn't that enough?" he asked angrily. "They saw the son of a bitch chase their mother with a shotgun. Isn't that enough?" his face was getting red.

"I understand how you feel Ryan. I love him, I can't help that. He said he's going to classes for anger management and it's only for a few hours. No one is going to be alone with him."

"You're crazy Kell. I would stay away from that bastard."

"Come on Ryan," said Rita. "He's her husband and besides, he's never been an ass during the day" she said laughing.

"Do what you want Kell, but you better be careful."

"I will" she replied and hugged her friends.

They shot several games of pool and talked with some friends. Kelly and Rita played the one armed bandit for a little while and they sank a lot of money in the juke box. Kelly and Rita were finishing the last lines of a Patsy Cline tune when Kelly looked up at the clock.

"Hey guys" Kelly said, "it's ten o'clock and I need to get back." "Okay, let me finish this beer and we're out of here" said Ryan. He chugged the last of his beer and the three friends left the bar. "I'm sorry if I sounded harsh in there" Ryan told her. "But damn it Kelly, you're my friend and I worry about you." "We both do" chimed Rita.

"I know, and that's why I love you guys." The driveway for Rita and Ryan was lit up like daylight. She pulled in and let her two friends out. "Let us know how it went Sunday" said Rita. "Yeah" said Ryan. "I need to know whether or not I'll need to kick his ass." "I love you too guys" was her reply and she backed slowly out of the driveway.

Kelly arrived home around ten thirty. "Where have you been?" asked her youngest daughter, Star. "Why are you out of bed?" Kelly asked with a smile. "It's ninety minutes past your bedtime."

"I was waiting for you. I had a nightmare" and she began to cry. "What was it about?" Kelly asked her as she drew her in close for a hug.

"It was monsters" she said with choked words from the tears.

"Monsters aren't real" Kelly reassured her.

"It felt like it was real" Star sobbed. "Can I sleep with you tonight?" her little face streaked with tears and her nose beginning to run.

"Let's get you cleaned up, and then you can sleep with me. But only for tonight, Ok?" Kelly said as she hugged her little girl.

"Ok. I was really scared."

"I know you were" Kelly said as they walked into the bathroom. Kelly dampened a washcloth with warm water and cleaned up Star's little face. They then walked into Kelly's room and she picked her little girl up and put her on the bed. Kelly pulled the covers down on the opposite side and Star crawled under. She kissed her mommy goodnight and hugged her then turned to face the wall and fell asleep that fast.

Kelly slipped in to the bathroom to take a shower and kill the smell of cigarettes emitting from her hair and skin. She dropped her clothes in the laundry basket and started the water for her shower. She washed her hair twice thinking that she could still smell smoke and then conditioned it, rinsed and climbed out after turning the water off.

She pulled a thin towel off the towel rack because she hated using thick towels. They just never made her feel completely dry. She brushed her hair and put on her lotion. Kelly put on her nightshirt and turned down the covers on her side. She crawled in the bed and pulled her covers on and tried to fall asleep. Her mind was racing with thoughts of Eric. She thought about Ryan's reaction to her taking the kids to see him and whether or not she really should.

Kelly closed her eyes and her mind filled with images of Eric chasing her with the shotgun and swinging the machete at her throat. Maybe she was out of her mind she thought but maybe he really has changed. Fifteen minutes later she was fast asleep . . . But it was a restless sleep.

Kelly's mind was filled with all sorts of tormented thoughts. She was in a deep sleep in a dream that felt extremely real. Her dreams took her back to when she was with Justin. She could see herself in the kitchen as though she were a third-party. She could feel the cold laminated floor beneath her bare feet and she could feel the gun pressed against her temple.

She could see herself begging Justin. Although she could hear the words they sounded as though they were coming from a distance and they did not sound like they were coming from her own voice. She sounded like a child while she was pleading for her life "Justin please, Please don't kill me I'll do anything you say, I'll do anything you ask Justin, please, please don't pull the trigger. I'm begging you Justin please put the gun down and I'll leave I promise! I swear I'll leave. I'll never come back Justin just please let me go."

The dream faded from Justin and turned into Eric. It was all like a haze. A haze that seemed to be clouding her mind. She could see Eric plain as day. He had the shotgun in his hand chasing her around the house. Kelly was screaming over her shoulder "Eric please, please don't kill me. I swear I'll listen to you I promise I'll listen to you but Eric please, please don't kill me."

Kelly woke in a full panic. She had sweat dripping from her temples, tears streaming down her face and her heart was racing. It took her a few minutes to realize that she was in her own bed in her own home and that there was no one there to harm her. She felt Star's little body move. Kelly realized she really was in her bed and in her own room. She breathed a sigh of relief, got out of bed and went into her bathroom closing the door behind her. She turned on the sink and splashed some water on her face. She patted her face dry with a towel and went back to bed. Although she thought it would take forever to go back to sleep it really only took her a few minutes. The rest of the night she tossed and turned but there were no more dreams.

CHAPTER THREE

Saturday morning was gray. The clouds were forming slowly and threatening rain. I hope it doesn't rain Kelly was thinking to herself. That would not be good. Sarah, her second to the oldest daughter came in the kitchen door. "I fed the horses for you mom and the chickens too."

"Thank you sweetie" she said to her.

Sarah stuck her beautiful blond hair behind her ears and said "I thought you could use the sleep."

"You are so thoughtful." Kelly smiled brightly. What beautiful and good hearted kids she has she thought to herself. "Get your hair from behind your ears" she told her.

"Mother, what is wrong with you? My ears will not stick out."

"I didn't say they would" Kelly said laughing.

"No, but you were thinking it" Sarah said smiling. "I know your thoughts mother."

"You always make me smile." Looking toward the living room, Kelly asked "are your sisters up yet? I know Star is, she slept in my bed last night."

"That's too funny" Sarah said smiling. "She slept in mine the night before. I know she was waiting for you when you got in" she laughed.

"Yes she was" Kelly said smiling. "She told me she had a nightmare. Now back to the subject at hand, are your sisters up?" she asked laughing.

"They are. They're watching TV in my room."

"Wow! It's not even eight thirty and they are all up. Will wonders never cease?" Kelly said laughing. "I'm going to make pancakes for breakfast, tell your sisters that breakfast will be ready in thirty minutes, ok?"

"I will. Did you have fun with your friends?"

"Yes" she said with a smile. "And we have something to talk about at breakfast."

"What is it? Did something happen?"

"At breakfast" she said smiling. "Now go tell your sisters when we're going to eat."

"Okay" Sarah said walking away. "Do you want help?"

"No, I'm good. Thank you though."

"You're welcome" and Sarah walked down the hall toward her room.

Breakfast was great! They were eating blueberry pancakes with blueberry syrup. "Sarah said you wanted to talk to us about something" her oldest daughter Rhonda said. "I do. Your dad wants to see you tomorrow." The excitement was great. They all began bombarding her with questions at the same time. "Slow down, one at a time" Kelly said. "You go first Rhonda."

"I'm not going. First of all he's not my dad, he's my stepdad and second of all, I have plans."

"You don't know when it is" Kelly said.

"You said tomorrow and I'm booked up for tomorrow."

"Not me" said Star eagerly. "I want to see daddy."

"He's an idiot too" Rhonda told her.

"I don't care he's my daddy and I miss him."

"He's going to make pizza" Kelly told them.

"I'll go for the pizza" said Lily. I love his pizza."

"Me too," Sarah and Star said in unison. Rhonda was shaking her head. "You do what you want, but I'm not going" she said firmly.

"That's your choice. I'm not going to force you to go," Kelly told her.

"Thank you. I appreciate your consideration for my feelings" she said while getting out of her chair. Rhonda ran her slender fingers through her long brown hair and closed her eyes for a second before saying "I can't believe that you are" her voice was filled with disgust. She walked away from the kitchen, her face flushed with anger.

"Why doesn't Rhonda want to go?" asked Star. "Doesn't she like daddy anymore?"

"Yes, she does. She has a boyfriend now and I think that's a little more important to her right now" Kelly answered. She let out a deep breath and ran her fingers through her dark brown hair. She could feel the tears threatening to come, but refused to let them. She knew exactly why Rhonda didn't want to go.

"I want you girls to go brush your teeth and make your beds. After that, I would like some help cleaning up."

"No" cried Lily. "I don't want to clean I want to get on the computer."

"You are going to help and that's final" said Kelly sternly.

"I'll help you mommy" Star told her.

"Thank you baby girl" Kelly replied and kissed her on her forehead.

"I'll help you too mother" said Sarah chiming in.

"Thank you too sweetie. Now go do what I said." The girls left the kitchen and walked down the long hall.

Sarah, Lily and Star returned about five minutes later. "Where's Rhonda?" Kelly asked the girls.

"We don't know" said Sarah.

"Probably in her room" Lily said.

"Star, you wash the dishes. Sarah, you sweep the floor and Lily, you can dry and put away the dishes. Don't forget to wipe the stove and the table. I've already washed the skillet."

Star grabbed a dishcloth and began her task while Sarah got the broom out. Lily waited beside the dish drainer for the first dish.

Kelly walked down the hall to Rhonda's room. She turned the knob and walked in. "Hey!" said Rhonda. "Don't you believe in knocking?"

"I told all of you to come back to the kitchen to help clean up" Kelly said harshly.

"I must not have been in there for that part because I don't remember hearing it" Rhonda retorted with the same level of harshness in her tone.

"What is your problem? I have always been able to count on you."

"You, you are my problem. He called Aunt Rita and Uncle Ryan to pick you up or he was going to kill you. Now you're going to take them over there to see him? Have you bumped your head mother?" The anger was flashing in Rhonda's sparkling hazel eyes. She ran her fingers through her hair and held them there for a second.

Kelly could feel the tears burning the back of her eyes. "No, I have not bumped my head."

"Have you forgotten what he did that night? I haven't, I remember everything he said and did. I remember him calling your best friend and telling her to come get us, or you were dead. What about that mother?"

"I remember it vividly Rhonda. He told me he has been going to meetings and he is trying to straighten himself out. He wants to see all of you. He wants to make a pizza and see you for a couple hours."

"Well, he's not my dad and I'm not going. If they are stupid enough to want to see him after what he did in there room, well that's up to them. I don't want to see the son of a bitch again." Rhonda's tone was determined.

"I'm not going to force you to see him. This is hard on everyone. Your sisters miss him and want to see him. I don't really believe he's changed, that's why I'm doing this in the daytime. Leopards don't change their spots" Kelly said wiping her eyes. "This is no picnic for me. I haven't forgotten a thing. But if I hadn't sent the pictures to Melody's phone, then maybe things would have been different."

"Yes mom, he would still be sneaking around the house getting high with his friends and you would be running after him chasing him outside. Is that really the kind of life you want to live? Hell mom, before you even got married he was an ass to you, or did you forget that as well?"

"No Rhonda, I didn't forget. I was making this their first and final visit. I know in my heart and in my mind he will never change. Your sisters need closure. They need to say goodbye to him sober."

"So you're not contemplating going back to him?" Rhonda asked, lowering her voice.

"No. I won't say that I don't wonder what life would have been like if things had been different, but I'm not deluding myself."

Rhonda walked over to her mother and wrapped her arms around her neck and hugged her. Kelly wrapped her arms around her daughter's thin frame and stroked her hair. The tears fell down both their cheeks. "I love you" Kelly told her.

"I love you too" she cried.

"So why don't you come help me clean the living room?"

The two broke their embrace and began to smile. "Ok" Rhonda said and they walked out of the room together.

CHAPTER FOUR

The sun was shining through the window pane. Kelly looked at the clock. Nine thirty. She had slept later than she planned to today. "Why didn't I set the alarm?" she thought to herself. She went to the kitchen and put the coffee on. She needed to call the girls so they could eat a quick breakfast and get ready for church.

Kelly's palms were moist. She hadn't anticipated how nervous she would be. Three and a half hours until she was supposed to have the kids at their old house. She had a strong feeling of dread. "Stop this" she chided herself. "You are making mountains out of molehills" and tried to smile.

Kelly grabbed a couple of boxes of cereal out of the cabinet and set some bowls and spoons on the table. She then went down the hall and called the girls to get up for breakfast. Church is in an hour and twenty minutes.

"Why did you call me so late?" asked Star as she sleepily walked out of her room.

"Yeah mom what's with the short notice for getting ready? I need to do my hair" complained Sarah pushing a stray strand of her long blond hair behind her ear.

Lily walked out of her room and straight into the bathroom. "Hey!" called Sarah. "I need in there first."

"I'm using the bathroom if you don't mind. Then you can get ready" Lily called through the door.

"Where's Rhonda?" asked Star.

"Sleeping" Kelly said simply and headed toward the kitchen.

"Isn't she going to church with us?"

"Since when does Rhonda attend church with us?" Kelly asked her with a smile.

"There's always a first time" Star retorted happily.

"Well, I don't think it will be this time. Besides, your sister used to go to church."

"Why doesn't she now?"

"She changed as she grew up. A different style of friends, personal choices, I really don't know. But, I respect her enough to let her make her own decisions."

"Well I like church and I want to keep going."

"And you can baby girl" Kelly told her giving her a long hug. "Now get moving we don't have a lot of time to get ready."

Kelly walked into the kitchen and poured a cup of coffee then walked out to the back deck. She looked at the horses frolicking in the pasture. What a beautiful sight to behold.

She wanted to drop everything and just saddle up and ride. Unfortunately, that wasn't on this morning's agenda. She had to get the animals fed and watered. When she finished, Kelly walked back inside to get showered and dressed for church. She needed to be there today, she could feel it.

Kelly chose a navy blue dress and watched Joel Osteen while she got ready. She loved Joel Osteen. She wondered why all preachers weren't like him then thought if they were, then he wouldn't be different. The world was blessed to have someone like him to guide them.

He was speaking about achieving your goals. Kelly drank in every word and knew she had to move forward in her life. She would take the kids to see their dad and say their goodbyes, but this would be the end.

They arrived at church a few minutes early. Star led the way inside and grabbed a program for everyone. They took a seat in one of the pews near the Olsen sisters. They exchanged greetings and had time to catch up on a few happenings before the preacher came in.

Kelly loved their preacher. She was a very kind and good hearted person. Not the pretentious type she had known before. No, their preacher was honest and gave you hope. She made it easy to understand the scripture.

The lesson today was about hope. They all listened intently. Kelly knew each member of the congregation would interpret the message differently, but not all people come to the same conclusions.

When the last hymn had been sung and the congregation was preparing to leave, Kelly and her girls took their places in line to give their goodbyes and thanks.

"It was a very informative sermon today" Kelly told Pastor Thompson. "We really enjoyed it. I especially learned a lot from that today." Kelly was smiling brightly.

"I'm so glad to hear that Kelly" Pastor Thompson told her. "I have been worried about you. I keep you all in my prayers. How are things going with you dear?" she asked with genuine concern.

"They are going good" Kelly smiled as she spoke. "I am taking the kids to see Eric today and say their proper goodbyes.

"Please be careful."

"I will. I finally know in my heart it's over. I still love him and I will for a while, but I know in my heart of hearts that I can't trust him."

"Just make sure you're careful. My thoughts and prayers will be with all of you. I love you."

"I love you too" Kelly replied with a tear in her eye.

The girls all gave Pastor Thompson a hug and a kiss on the cheek and told her they would see her next Sunday. Kelly and the girls walked out into the beautiful sunshine and got in the car to head for home.

Are we going to daddy's now?" asked Star. "No, I'm taking you home to change, then we will go to daddy's house" Kelly told her.

She must have been satisfied with that answer because she settled down in her seat without protest. As they pulled in the drive, they saw a dark blue pickup truck parked there.

"Who's that?" everyone asked at once and then broke into laughter.

"I guess we'll find out when we walk inside" Kelly said still laughing.

"I guess we will" said Sarah. They went inside and were introduced to Rhonda's friends Mark and Jeff.

"We're going to play video games, ok mom?" said Rhonda.

"Sure. It was nice to meet you both. There are leftovers in the fridge if you get hungry. We are getting ready to leave."

"Thanks mom" Rhonda said, hugging her mother. "See you when you get back. Please be careful."

"I will" she told her and walked back to her room.

Kelly and the girls changed their clothes and headed to Eric's. The pizza was already prepared when they got there and he had cokes to drink. The girls were really happy with the pizza.

He hugged each of the girls and then Kelly. After the girls were finished with their meals, Eric told them he was tired from working late and needed a nap. They hugged him again and said goodbye. Each of them told him they loved him and thanked him for their lunch.

He walked over to hug Kelly. "I still love you babe" he told her. She looked in his big brown eyes and touched his curly brown hair.

"I love you too" she said quietly.

"Then why don't you and the kids come back home?" he asked, his voice sort of a croak.

"I can't do that. I need to move on Eric. We love each other, but we just can't get along."

"Would you please come by at eight? We have a lot of things we need to talk about. Like if you want a divorce?" he said in question tone.

"I don't know if that's a good idea Eric."

"You owe me that much Kelly. You've been gone a couple months. I would like a chance to at least give my side. You owe me that much."

"I would think you owe that to me" Kelly said dryly.

"Maybe I do, but please, won't you please come?" He looked so sad that Kelly felt sorry for him. All the torment that he had put her through eluded her mind.

"Okay, I'll be here at eight."

"Great, I'll see you then" he said with a broad smile on his face. Then he hugged the girls one last time and put them in the car. "Be good for your mom" he told them and closed the door. "I'll see you at eight" he told Kelly with a smile.

"See you then" she said. They were all quiet on the drive home.

CHAPTER FIVE

Kelly chose to wear black jeans with a blue silk blouse and high heeled black boots. She didn't want to overdress because she didn't want to give him the wrong impression. She also didn't want to dress down because she wanted him to see what he had chosen to throw away.

Rhonda didn't want her to go. She was really afraid for her mom. "I don't trust him mom! I think he has something planned. I really have a bad feeling about this." Rhonda was pleading with her mother. She tried to sway her mother's mind but that just wasn't going to happen.

"I'm going to hear what he has to say. I need closure Rhonda. I would also prefer to settle things out of divorce court rather than in it" she said, her throat feeling dry. Kelly walked to the sink and got a glass of water.

"Whatever, it's your funeral. Don't say I didn't warn you about the jackass. Remember when you were dating and he grabbed the steering wheel of your car and headed us into traffic because he thought some guy looked at you too long? Remember when you were dating and he had the music up really loud one night and you went out and told him to turn it down? Remember how he chased you with a machete?" Rhonda's eyes were burning with tears and anger was seeping through her. "I do! I had to hide you in my room. You still married him mom. Even though he was showing signs then that he was an abuser."

"I remember all of that and more baby girl. But I have to talk this out once and for all. I need to see how we can settle this like adults and not through court. He said he has changed and I have to give him the benefit of the doubt."

"I can't believe you are still going. It's like you are blind or oblivious to his actions. What has to happen next mom for you to think straight?" and with that said Rhonda stomped back to her room.

Kelly grabbed her jacket and walked out of the door. She put the key in the ignition and chided herself for being so stubborn. She then told herself that she wasn't being stubborn, she was going to negotiate a divorce.

Kelly started the car and backed out of the driveway. She put the car in drive and was on her way. Her mind was racing a mile a minute. "What if he really has changed? No he hasn't, he is the same as always. Am I really doing the right thing? Should I go over there alone?" The thoughts were racing through her mind.

"He was sober when you let him see the girls. He wouldn't be drunk already. He asked you to come over he wouldn't want to mess it up. No, he wants to make a good impression because he asked you to come home" Kelly spoke aloud.

She turned on the radio and began to sing along. It was beginning to take her mind off of things when she arrived at her destination. Nervously she put the car in park and turned off the ignition. She got out holding her keys in her hand. She checked her makeup in the rear view mirror and added some lip gloss. She smiled at herself and said "Here you go girl I hope you know what you're doing." She grabbed her purse and got out of the car.

The smell of smoke filled the air. "Eric must be burning trash" she thought and walked up the steps to the door. She knocked on the door because she didn't want to just walk in.

Eric stood there smiling. It was a strange smile, neither friendly nor angry. He opened the door and said "Hey there, come in. I didn't think you would show."

"I told you I would be here" she said cautiously, as she stepped inside.

"Yes but you say a lot of things you don't mean" and he waited by the kitchen door as he ushered her toward the living room. Kelly couldn't help but notice the huge fire burning outback. She couldn't miss it through the window. That explains the smell she thought.

"What do you mean by that Eric?" she asked worriedly. This was not feeling very good.

"Our wedding vows for one. You promised to love, honor and obey 'til death we do part and you didn't keep that one." He took a seat on the sofa in front of the coffee table where he had a trash can and his wallet.

"I kept our vows Eric. I have never cheated or ran around."

"You left and didn't want to come back."

"Eric, you told me to leave. You called Rita and Ryan and told them to come get me and the girls before you killed me."

"I should not have done that."

Kelly looked around the room nervously. The front windows had trash bags taped over them and boards nailed across that and the front door had three boards nailed across it.

Eric sat there sweating bullets. He was dumping the ashtray into the trash can and then digging the cigarette butts out and putting them back. He would then take the money and cards from his wallet and throw them away and then retrieve them from the trash.

"I thought we would watch a movie and talk about things. I can come back another time if that suits you better."

"Why don't you get me another beer?"

"Ok. Are you alright, you look a little warm." Kelly was beginning to feel extremely nervous. She noticed from the back window that it was beginning to rain again. They had been having heavy downpours all day on and off today. At least it wasn't raining when they went to church and it hadn't started again until she got home from Eric's with the kids.

"Are you going to get me that beer or am I going to thirst to death?"

"I'm getting it" she said nervously. "What movie would you like to watch?" she asked as she grabbed a beer from the fridge.

"I'm not watching a movie. Man you ask a lot of freaking questions." Eric was starting to sound very aggravated. "Sit down, you're making me nervous. What did you do? Call the cops on me or something?" Eric asked angrily.

"No I have never called the police on you." Kelly was really nervous now. Her heart was racing and she couldn't leave through the front door with it being boarded up.

"Are you going to move back home?" Eric asked sharply.

"I told you no. I thought you wanted to talk. I thought you wanted to settle things outside of a divorce. I can't live like this anymore." she told him.

"Maybe you don't need to live." The look in his eyes was dark, sinister almost.

"That's not funny Eric. You're high again aren't you?" she asked nervously.

"What is your freaking problem?" he shouted. "What's it to you? You don't live here anymore remember? You left like a freaking traitor."

"You see? This is why we can't get along. You can't stop getting high." Kelly was beginning to feel angry tears threatening her. She did not want to let them fall. "Look, just let me get the rest of my things and I'll leave you alone."

"You don't have anything."

"What is that supposed to mean? Almost all of my clothes are here."

"Your clothes are outback on that burn pile" he said laughing wickedly.

"No Eric! You didn't, you wouldn't!"

"I did you lousy bitch. I knew I couldn't count on you to keep your vows, in sickness and in health, for better or worse Kelly. Now you're running around like a two bit whore."

"You made me leave Eric" she pleaded. "And I've never run around." She could see the look of anger in his eyes. It was flashing clearly. How could she have missed every sign and warning that had led up to this? She thought to herself.

"You have a few things in the bedroom, you can have those." Eric said that with complete calm, showing no emotion.

"Fine, I'll get them and leave" she said as she walked through the threshold into the kitchen.

"No you won't bitch." Eric was turning fast and she needed to gain control of this situation.

"Just let me have what's left of my things, ok Eric?" she pleaded softly. She looked around the kitchen and noticed that the back door was also boarded shut. "Please?" she added softly.

"Fine" he said. "Get your shit and get the hell out. You're an ungrateful bitch" he said.

"I'm sorry Eric, I never meant to upset you" she said beginning to cry. She blinked her eyes hard to stop the tears and walked toward the bedroom with Eric on her heels.

Kelly picked up a backpack and began putting some of her knickknacks in it. Eric stood directly behind her watching her every move. He walked up behind her and moved her hair off the side of her neck. She could feel the warmth of his breath and smell the beer he had been drinking. He started kissing her neck and rubbing her arms and then placed his hands on her stomach as his kisses became harder.

"Stop Eric, please stop" Kelly begged, the tears beginning to stream down her face.

"Come on Kell, one last time. Please, let me show you how much I love you, what you are missing. Let me show you how I've changed."

"That's just it, you haven't changed Eric. You still think making love makes all of our problems go away" she cried.

"You know how good it is after a fight. Tell me you don't enjoy it and I'll leave you alone. I'll know it's over and you can take your things and leave" he said as he placed more kisses on her neck and turned her to face him so his lips could meet hers.

Kelly's thoughts were going a mile a minute. "I have to stop this she told herself, before I give in." Kelly put her hands on Eric's shoulders pushing him back to break the kiss.

"No, Eric! This is not what I'm here for. We were supposed to watch a movie and talk settlement out of court. I'm not having sex with you no matter how good or bad it is." Kelly regretted her words immediately.

"You lousy psycho bitch" he said, a crazed look in his eyes.

Kelly remembered how many times he had called her that in the past. She knew now that she struck a wrong cord and needed to smooth things over quickly. "I'm sorry Eric. I didn't mean that the way it sounds."

"You meant every word you said. Remember Kelly, you don't lie, you don't break your vows" he said in an almost inaudible whisper. "Get your shit and get the hell out of my house" he screamed.

She started to do exactly as he said. Kelly picked up her beach bag and Eric went nuts. "Don't touch that" he screamed.

"Why not, it's mine" she said, her hands trembling and her voice shaking.

"I have something in there" he screamed at her. Eric stood between Kelly and the door. She could not escape if she tried to run and she was frightened.

CHAPTER SIX

Kelly tried to keep her wits. She handed the bag to him thinking that it would give her a means of escape. Eric took the bag from her and searched it. He stood planted in front of her.

Kelly tried to pass by him and he drew back his right hand and swung back handing her. The force was heavy lifting her off of her feet and knocking her into the closet. As Kelly tried to regain her breath fear filled her very being. "God please let me get out of here alive" she prayed.

Kelly tried to get to her feet and stumbled. Eric threw the bag into her chest. "Here" he said. "Where's my shit? You stole my freaking shit."

"I didn't take anything" she stammered, but before she could say another word, Eric punched her in the chest sending her backward across their king sized bed and into the other closet. She tried to get herself back up after the heavy blow, but she could not catch her breath. Fear was taking over her body and she needed to calm down. The pain emanating from her chest was excruciating.

Eric walked over and picked her up by her hair. He then drew back his left hand and let it fly across Kelly's already swelling face. Kelly could taste the blood coming from inside her lip where Eric had hit her. She felt as though she could taste blood with every breath she exhaled.

"Eric please" she begged and he drew back his right arm again, grabbing her with his left hand and backhanded her back across the bed. The blood from her mouth was covering her chin and Kelly could not get her breath. Eric had knocked the wind out of her. Her breathing slowly came back as Eric was walking around the bed toward her, pure hatred in his eyes. She was screaming for help but no sound was emitting from her mouth.

Eric caught her ankle and jerked her to the floor. She felt his fist hit her back. She thought he drove it straight through her body. The mind numbing pain was excruciating. She felt her blouse rip as he tried yanking her back toward him. Kelly desperately tried to crawl away from him, kicking her feet as hard as she could in his direction. She felt her belt loop snap next as he grabbed at her pants to pull her toward him. She desperately kicked back connecting with his chest and getting to crawl away from him. She was screaming for help as loudly as she could. "Could anyone hear her?" she thought as she tried to steal a look through a boarded window. She could hear the sounds of the storm outside.

How was anyone ever going to hear her cries for help with that storm outside, she asked herself. She managed to get to the kitchen, kicking at Eric to keep him at bay.

The rain poured and the thunder raged. Kelly knew the storm wouldn't allow any passersby to hear the screams coming from inside that little home. She finally made it to the kitchen. She quickly scanned it for an escape.

The door was locked with a dead bolt. Kelly knew she could never escape Eric. Tears were streaming down her thin face. Her eyes more piercing blue from the reddened whites. The bruises were already beginning to show. She was pleading with Eric to just let her go.

Eric had grabbed her by her hair and dragged her backward. The pain was fierce, but not as fierce as the pain in her chest and back. Kelly began kicking wildly hoping to connect with his crotch so she could escape. She struck a blow on his inner thigh and he let go of her hair. She tripped and he grabbed her by her ankles.

"I won't tell anyone Eric, I promise" she pleaded choking on her tears and shortness of breath. The pain was fierce. Kelly managed to kick her way free of Eric, his fingers digging deep into her ankles as she retrieved them from his grasp. She made it back to the kitchen.

She reached for the phone from the kitchen wall in desperate hopes of calling 911. As her trembling hands punched the numbers on the keypad, he ripped the phone cord from the wall. "He's going to kill me and there's no one who can save me now" thought Kelly. "God, please let me get out of here alive," she silently prayed.

Eric hit her hard across her face busting the other side of her lips. "Eric, please, please, Eric" she cried desperately. "Please let me go. What would your father do if you kill me?" "It won't look good for reelection time Eric" she pleaded.

Eric turned the deadbolt on the door and picked Kelly up throwing her with all his might down the stairs. Kelly landed hard into her car parked in front of the door. "God please don't let him kill me. I promise I won't go back" she cried. She felt a horrific pain as her beach bag connected with her back.

The pouring rain made it hard for her to grip the car. Eric threw Kelly's purse down the stairs at her. Kelly grabbed her purse and beach bag. She struggled to get her keys but was glad she had put them in it after walking inside.

Eric came running down the steps as Kelly reached her keys. He had a knife in his hand, a long bladed butcher's knife. Kelly clicked the unlock button and just made it in the car and had time to lock the door when Eric reached her. She grabbed her cell phone she left on the console. She put her key in the ignition and started her car so that the phone would charge.

Eric began screaming obscenities at her through the closed window. "Open the door you bitch" he screamed. "You freaking psycho bitch." He looked like a madman as he pressed his face against the window. He had a long bladed knife in his right hand as he said "I don't want to hurt you I just want to kill you no good lousy bitch. You're a traitor Kelly!"

Frantically, Kelly dialed 911. The woman whom answered the phone asked "what is your emergency?"

"My husband has a knife, he's trying to kill me" Kelly stammered into the phone.

"I'm going to kill you, you bitch" Eric screamed while beating on the window of the little car.

"Ma'am, who is that in the background?" the operator asked.

"That's my husband. He's going to break the glass. He's going to kill me" Kelly cried choking on her tears.

"Do you have someplace to go?"

"Yes, but I need help now. He's holding on to my car. He's going to break my window. He's going to kill me."

"Ma'am what is your location?"

Kelly told the 911 operator her location.

"Ma'am, your roads are flooded and we can't get an officer out to you" the operator told her. "Please leave and call me at your destination." Worry sounded in her voice.

"I need help, I need an ambulance" Kelly insisted.

"Ma'am" the operator said. "I sympathize with you but I can't get anyone out to you. Can you drive?"

"Yes but I can barely breathe. And I'm bleeding so hard." Kelly was terrified. The sounds of Eric beating the car window were coming through the phone. "I'm going to kill you bitch" he said with pure venom.

"Leave now!" said the operator. "An officer can meet you seven miles at the Gas Way" she said urgently. "Please go!"

Kelly dropped the gear shift in reverse and floored the little engine. Gravel flew as she rolled backward. Eric was holding tight to her door. His fingers finally let loose of the door and he began running behind her screaming profanities and throwing rocks at the car.

When Kelly's wheels were on the road surface, she dropped the car in drive and floored her again. The little car sped away from the ugly scene without hesitation. Kelly's phone lost signal but she headed toward the gas station to meet the officer.

The water was deep. Kelly didn't think she would make it through. Her little car started to choke and Kelly began to panic. The water level was about midway to her wheels and beginning to seep in under the door.

She trudged the water for two miles and the flooding was then at a tolerable level. Another two miles and the flooding was minimal. Kelly's cell phone rang. It was the 911 operator. "I have been trying to get you" she said.

"I lost my signal" Kelly cried into the receiver.

"I have a state trooper waiting for you at the Gas Way" she said.

"Thank you" Kelly said tears streaming down her face mixing with blood. "I think I'm going to pass out, I'm really dizzy" she said.

"You can make it. You made it out of that house didn't you?" the operator said with sympathy.

"Yes I did" Kelly said sniffling. She wiped her nose on the back of her sleeve and was wiping her eyes with her hand. "I see the Gas Way in front of me" Kelly said.

"I am informing the trooper right now. Do you see him?"

"Yes, I do. He has his lights on." Kelly was crying harder. She didn't know how to control her tears. She couldn't stop sobbing.

"It's ok" said the operator. "You're a survivor. You are safe now. Have you reached the trooper?"

"Yes, he's walking to my car." Her voice was barely audible.

"Alright, I'm going to hang up now, you're in good hands. Everything will be ok" the operator reassured her.

"Thank you" Kelly told her, "Thank you very much."

"No problem" replied the operator and she dropped the line.

CHAPTER SEVEN

The trooper approached the car. Kelly lowered the window. When the trooper saw the condition of Kelly's face he called for an ambulance.

"Can you tell me what happened miss?" the Trooper asked.

"My husband and I are separated and he invited me over to talk" Kelly said gasping for air.

"Ma'am, take it easy. Slow down and take your time." The Trooper's tone was very soothing.

"He had all the doors nailed shut. He hit me several times in my chest knocking me backwards and punched me in the back. He back handed me a couple times. He grabbed me by my ankles and wouldn't let me near the phone. He threw me down the steps and tried to beat the windows out of my car to get to me" Kelly cried. She was beginning to sob hysterically.

The Trooper noticed small cracks in the window of the driver side of the car. He has got to be one strong monster the trooper thought to himself.

"Can you tell me how your clothes came to be torn?" he asked in a gentle tone.

"My, my husband did it" she sobbed.

The Trooper looked at her with sympathetic eyes and secretly wished he could have driven out to her house and seen the monster face to face. This woman was maybe 5 foot four and a hundred five pounds if that. What the hell was wrong with men these days? The trooper noticed the flashing lights entering the parking lot.

"The ambulance is here now. We will get you to the hospital and get you checked out."

The paramedic came running toward Kelly's car with a medical bag in hand and a stethoscope around her neck. "Hi sweetie, my name is Terri and I'm going to take your vitals. Can you sit up for me?" she asked in a soft tone.

"Yes" she replied, still sobbing. "But it really hurts when I do."

"You need to calm down. I know you must have been through a lot, but I really need you to try to calm down." She placed the stethoscope on Kelly's back and told her to take a deep breath. Kelly almost screamed as she tried to do it.

The Trooper picked up Kelly's hand and held it, patting it lightly and softly talking to her, telling her that it was all going to be alright. The driver came running up to the car and Kelly let out a scream as she saw the six foot two inch man.

"Noooo, don't let him near me, don't let him near me" Kelly screamed. "Please, please don't let Eric hurt me again."

She began blocking her face as though she were about to be hit. The terror was clearly showing in her eyes.

"That's not Eric" the Trooper said patting her hand. That is the ambulance driver. Does he look like Eric?" Kelly nodded. "Is Eric your husband?"

"Yes, please don't let him near me. He's going to kill me." The look in her eyes was that of a terrified child. It was heart breaking. She was shaking all over and the rain continued to pour.

"Ma'am, I need to take your blood pressure but I would rather do that on our way to the hospital" Terri told her. "The tall gentleman over there is our driver. He is not going to hurt you. He is bringing the stretcher so we can get you loaded up." Terri's tone was soothing.

"Okay," she said. Just please don't let Eric find me." Then Kelly looked horrified. "My kids oh please my kids. Somebody please check my kids."

"Are your children at the house with your husband ma'am?" the Trooper asked with alarm.

"No, no they are at my farm. Can someone please make sure Eric doesn't hurt them?"

"What's the number? I can call and let you speak to them" he told her.

"Thank you. It's 555-2320. Ask for Rhonda, she's the oldest. Please make sure they are okay." Her eyes looked so haunted and desperately pleading, the Trooper couldn't turn away. He dialed the number on his cell as the attendants readied her for transport.

The phone was answered on the third ring. "Hello" said a sleepy voice.

"This is Trooper Fielder, may I speak with Rhonda?" he asked the voice.

"This is she. Oh no," Rhonda said with alarm "has something happened to my mom? I told her not to go over there. I told her it was all a ploy. I told her he was going to kill her." The girl was talking so fast that Fielder couldn't get a word in.

"Slow down, slow down. We are with your mom and she is going to the hospital to get checked out."

"Is it bad?" Rhonda cried into the receiver.

"She is heading to the hospital now. I will call you with an update. Is everything okay at your house?" he asked concerned.

"Yes, why wouldn't it be?" Rhonda asked surprised by the question.

"Just making sure ma'am, keep your doors and windows locked and don't answer them. Is there someone that you can call to come and sit with you until your mother gets back?" he asked.

"My Aunt Rita and Uncle Ryan, I can call them" she said beginning to cry.

"Try to hold it together Rhonda. I need you to stay focused and watch out for the other children. I want you to call your Aunt Rita and Uncle Ryan the minute I get off the phone. Can you do that? Can you have them come and sit with you? Your mom may be a while" then rethinking his choice of words he added "you know how slow hospitals are."

"I'll do it right now. Will you tell my mom I love her please?" she asked crying.

"Can do, now make that call" he said and closed his phone.

They loaded Kelly onto a stretcher and put her in the ambulance. "Your daughter said to tell you she loves you" Trooper Fielder told her. Kelly tried to smile through the apparatus on her face that was putting out the oxygen she needed. It was halfhearted.

Although the ride to the hospital was only ten minutes, it seemed like an hour to Kelly. It was getting harder and harder to breathe. The oxygen wasn't helping at all.

CHAPTER EIGHT

When the ambulance pulled into the hospital emergency room zone, the driver opened the door. The paramedic was already pulling the stretcher toward the door. Trooper Fielder was there to help pull the stretcher out of the ambulance.

They lowered the stretcher and wheeled her into the hospital. They gave the nurse Kelly's vitals and Trooper Fielder informed her of what happened.

They immediately took her to a room and the doctor walked straight in while they were transferring her to a hospital bed. "Hi, what's your name?"

"Kelly, Kelly Price" she stammered.

"Can you tell me what happened tonight?" he asked.

"My husband beat me." Kelly began. She then gave him every gruesome detail of her terrifying night. The doctor ordered x-rays of her neck, chest and back. A nurse came in and started an IV on her. "What's this for?" Kelly asked.

"In case we need to treat you or you need surgery" the nurse replied. "I have a list of allergies" Kelly told her.

"Has the doctor been informed?" the nurse asked her.

"I haven't informed him" Kelly said finding it still hard to breathe. With that a technician came down from the x-ray department to take her to x-ray.

The nurse said she would inform the doctor that she was headed to x-ray. The tech asked her what her pain level was and she replied a ten. When the x-rays were complete, they returned her to her room.

Kelly's tan face was now ghostly white from the pain that taking the deep breaths and holding them caused. She had to take them though for the x-rays. She was relieved when it was over.

The doctor came in to see her when he received the x-rays. "Mrs. Price you have 2 cracked ribs and a hairline fracture to your sternum. You also have a herniated disc at your C-4 and C-5 of your cervical spine. There is a lot of swelling in your back and shoulder and the image is not very clear. I think you are going to need an MRI when the swelling goes down. Right now it looks as though you could have a torn rotator cuff in your shoulder. To top it all off that lip is going to need a couple of stitches too. Do you mind if I check your back where he punched you?" the doctor asked. I really am not comfortable with the fact that the x-ray couldn't get a clear picture."

"Please do" she said a little breathlessly. "Are the rib and sternum the reason I can't breathe very well?" Kelly asked.

"Yes they are" he said. The doctor pressed the lower back on the right side. Kelly winced in pain. "I believe you also have a bruised kidney" he informed her. If I'm not mistaken, I believe you also have a broken sacrum." Turning to the attending nurse he said "bring me a kit, I need to stitch that lip."

"How long will it take to heal?" Kelly asked.

"It's going to take a long time. I would say at least six to eight weeks for the muscle injuries and three months or more for the sacrum. As far as the sternum is concerned, it could take at least a year. You also have a bruised chest wall. I mean how fast it heals, depends on how quickly your body heals the broken bones. I won't kid you it's going to be a long slow haul. The sternum and chest wall will take the longest because every time you breathe you pull it apart again" he told her looking her straight in the eyes. "I hear you have allergies" he said to her.

"Yes I do" she told him. "A lot of them" Kelly couldn't focus. It hurt so much to breathe.

"I really need to know these allergies" he said to Kelly and then turned to the nurse. "Why wasn't this covered in the ambulance or when she was admitted?" he asked sternly.

"Dr. Vance, I honestly don't have a reason other than she was so distraught she wasn't capable of answering anything." It made Kelly feel sorry for the nurse.

"I should wear an ID bracelet, but there are too many to fit on it" she said heavily as she tried hard to take a breath.

The nurse exited the room and returned momentarily with the kit. The doctor began preparing Kelly for her stitches. He wiped her lip with Betadine and was going to inject her with Lidocaine. "What's that?" Kelly asked horrified. "It's just some Lidocaine to numb your lip so we can stitch it" he told her gently.

"I can't have that" she told him. "I'm allergic to that and novacain."

"I really need to know your list of allergies" Doctor Vance told her.

"It's Lidocain, Lithocain, Novacain, aspirin, ibuprofen, penicillin vk, Tylenol three, Darvocet" Kelly went through the entire list.

"Is there anything you're not allergic to?" he asked in astonishment.

"That would have been a much easier list" Kelly replied trying to smile. "Acetaminophen, Amoxicillin, and Endocet. Those are the three"

"You are kidding, right?" asked Dr. Vance.

"I wish I were" Kelly replied. "You have to stich it raw Doc, I'm sorry."

"Please don't apologize to me sweetheart. You're the one that is about to endure some terrific pain."

"It's no worse than I have already been dealt this evening" she said trying to keep her voice from shaking.

"Can you take percosets?" He asked her.

"No, I get hives and wheezing from them" she told him. "I can only handle the Endocet."

"Ok, we are going to get you some."

"No not now. I will have to drive home and I can't take them and drive they make me dizzy and sleepy."

"Okay, I'll write you a prescription for those and some muscle relaxers.

"Unfortunately, I can't take those either" Kelly said trying not to start crying again.

I will send you home with two tablets because I know the pharmacy is closed. I'm sorry but I really need to stitch that lip now. I really wish I could give you something" he said wincing at the pain he knew he would cause on top of all her other pain.

He threaded the curved needle and began to stick it through her lip. Kelly's eyes shot wide with pain and fear and she let out a horrific scream. "I'm so sorry, but please try to remain calm" he told her. The Trooper could not look in her direction all he could think was that with everything this woman went through tonight, the nightmare still isn't over.

The doctor had to call in two orderlies and three additional nurses to help hold Kelly down. Deep in his mind he thought how horrifying this has to be to this poor woman lying here on this gurney.

The original nurse grabbed Kelly's left hand because of all the injuries on her right side and let her squeeze her hand. "There, there sweetie, it will all be over soon" she cooed. Kelly squeezed the nurse's hand tightly, trying her best not to scream. Her heart raced and the tears ran freely down her face. But the three nurses had held her arms and legs while the two orderlies held her head in place. Seven stitches later, it was over.

CHAPTER NINE

Dr. Vance patted Kelly's arm and looked as though he had a tear in his eye. He turned to the state trooper who was still in the room and said "I hope you arrested this man."

"As much as I would like to, I can't."

"What do you mean you can't?" cried Kelly frantically and sounding muffled through a stitched lip. "He tried to kill me."

"That's out of my hands. I can't arrest him because I was not at your house. I met you at a gas station. In order to arrest him, I have to see him in the act or you at the scene just after the act. You will have to file charges yourself with the commissioner. I have a pamphlet for you on domestic violence and I will have someone contact you. In the meantime, I would like you to go to the courthouse and file a protective order when they open at nine."

Kelly went completely pale. "So what you're telling me is that he is still out there and no one can keep me safe." The doctor was shaking his head in disapproval.

"Are you kidding me?" he asked in astonishment. "Do you see the condition of this patient?"

"Yes I do, but my hands are tied. The law states that if I did not witness or come to the home, I cannot make an arrest. I'm sorry. I'm truly sorry. If he bothers you again, don't hesitate to call."

"With all due respect, what good would it do? I called for you to come tonight but you couldn't because it was flooded. How will you get to me if he does it again? You won't. You won't be able too." Kelly began sobbing all over again.

The trooper reached in his wallet and handed Kelly his business card. "I will be there! Call me direct and I will be there. I took the liberty of writing my cell number on the back of this card. Now, if you don't mind, I need to take some pictures of your injuries to put with my report."

"That's fine" Kelly said exasperatedly and still sobbing.

As the trooper took his photos, the doctor left the room to fill out Kelly's discharge papers and instructions.

When the trooper was finished Kelly asked him if he would drive her back to her car. "I'm not supposed to, but I will."

"Thank you" she said with a weak smile, tears still streaming down her face. The nurse came in with the discharge instructions and went over everything with Kelly. "He gave you a note for work to cover you one week. He wants you in your primary's office then and he can write the note for longer. He also gave you two endocets to take home and a prescription for twenty eight more."

"Thank you" Kelly said and had the nurse help her down from the bed. "Tomorrow you will feel like a bus ran over you" she said.

"Thanks so much for all that you did for me. And just for the record, I already feel like a bus ran over me" Kelly said trying to joke but the pain was searing and her efforts were failing.

The trooper stepped outside the room so Kelly could dress. Noticing her ripped up shirt the nurse gave Kelly a hospital gown to wear home. When she was dressed, the trooper helped her walk out of the emergency department and to his car.

"I honestly wish I could do more for you" he told Kelly looking at her intently. "I am sorry that I can't." He helped her in his car and drove her to the gas station.

"Thank you" Kelly said with tears in her eyes. The pain was almost unbearable.

"You're welcome. Please call me if he comes back. I will get there no matter how high the water is." Kelly looked into his eyes and for the first time noticed how gray they were. The light reflecting from his head and around the brim of his hat told her he was bald or had a very close shaved head. He was very handsome Kelly thought and wondered how her mind could think those thoughts.

They arrived at Kelly's car and the trooper helped her to her car. "Thank you" Kelly said with tears brimming.

"You're welcome. Do you want me to follow you home?" he asked concern filling his voice.

"If you don't mind" Kelly replied. "What are you allowed to?" Kelly asked.

"Not really. I don't mind at all. I will just radio in and tell them I am looking for the suspect" he replied, smiling.

"I really appreciate that" she told him.

"By the way Mrs. Price, my name is Trooper Fielder, in case you didn't hear before" he told her and he walked away toward his car. Once inside his cruiser, he followed Kelly back to her house.

The trooper pulled in the driveway behind her. He stepped out of his cruiser and walked up to Kelly's door. She put her window down so he could speak to her. "If you need anything, please call" he told her.

"Thank you I will, but what if it's still flooded?" she asked pointedly, still looking like a frightened child.

"I'll just drive through it like I did following you here. I can't leave you with good conscience knowing that animal is out there. Please make sure you file those charges and the protective order."

"I will" she assured him and said goodnight which should have been good morning.

He held her door and took her hand and gently lifted her up. Her hair shone brightly even in the dim light of the dome and with blood mixed in.

Kelly grabbed her paper work from the hospital and her purse. The officer held on to her waist as he walked her to the door.

"I'm not hurting you, am I?" He asked with concern.

"No. Thank you for helping me walk" Kelly said to him. "I don't think I would have made it without you."

"It's the least I can do. I needed to be sure you got here safely. Please be careful" he told her gently but sternly.

"I will" she said. "Thank you again" Kelly said and the Trooper couldn't help but notice how vividly blue her eyes were. How could any man in his right man want to hurt a woman like that he thought. It takes a real monster to hit a woman.

"You're welcome. Remember to file for that protective order and the criminal charges" he said as he backed down the porch steps. "And you might want to get a dog" he said as an afterthought. "For your protection" he said. "And possibly a gun, but you didn't hear that from me."

"I believe I will on both counts" she said.

"By the way, my first name is Tom," he said with a smile.

"It's nice to meet you Tom, please call me Kelly" she said trying to smile and failing.

"Make sure you lock your doors Kelly and if you need me please don't hesitate to call." With that said, the trooper turned and headed towards his car.

When the trooper got in his car, Kelly turned the porch light off and locked the door. She went in the bathroom and took a shower. Kelly winced from the pain of water pelting on her bruised skin and muscles.

The face in the mirror as she brushed her hair was a horrible sight. "Now the fear begins" Kelly said to herself beginning to cry again and crawled into her bed. From here on out life wasn't going to be easy.

"Let the battle begin" she thought as she pulled up the sheets. "Our lives will never be the same again. God please grant me strength to do what needs to be done. I'm going to really need your help" she said looking up toward the ceiling with tears in her eyes.

Kelly lay awake several hours thinking of what to tell her kids, and came to the realization that she couldn't hide the truth.

Now she would know what it was like to live in hell she thought. What she had just gone through would only be the beginning once she filed those charges. "Who's going to save me now?" she thought aloud. "Life will never be the same. How could I let things get this bad? Why didn't I pay attention to the warning signs that were there all along" she bereted herself.

There was really no sense in reprimanding herself. She had loved him, she still did. Kelly tossed and turned in excruciating pain trying to find a comfortable position as she replayed the last four years in her mind trying to figure out what she could have done differently to have prevented it.

When she first met Eric he was so wonderful. He bought her roses and candy and he was so kind and gentle. There were a few times when they had fought because he was drinking too much and being too loud. Of course he was always jealous every time another man looked at her. She thought that was proof of how much he loved her. How many times had she had to stop him from getting in an altercation over her? How many times did he yell at her saying it was her fault because of the way she was dressed or because she was wearing too much makeup?

Kelly fought back the tears that were already threatening to fall. Were these the warning signs of possible domestic violence behavior? If these weren't then what were the signs? He wanted her to pull in to a bar a few different times and when she refused he grabbed the steering wheel while she was driving and steered her into oncoming traffic with the kids in the car too.

What about the times he had slapped her and her friends had all told her to stop seeing him, it would only escalate into something worse? How could she be so blind? Does love keep you from seeing the truth about a person or is it the fear of being alone? Why didn't she see this before? Was it because the sex was so good after he hurt her and was trying to prove he loved her? It was always better when he was making up for something he had done to her.

How can love be this blind? How could she not see the animal that everyone else had? All she had ever wanted was for someone to love her, especially after what she had gone through with Justin. How could this have happened to her twice in a row? Eric had been there for her after all that Justin had put her through. He even sat with her through every court hearing holding her hand and supporting her through it all.

Kelly's eyes were stinging with overflowing tears. She reached for a tissue from the box on her nightstand. Her throat ached from all the crying. Opening the nightstand drawer, Kelly reached in and grabbed out a Hall's cough drop to open up her nose. All this crying had it completely stuffed up. She got out of her bed slowly and walked over to the mirror on her dresser and took a good look at herself.

"This is what happens when you ignore the signs" she chided herself. "How could you be so stupid? You think you look bad now? Just wait until tomorrow or the next day or the day after that! What are your children going to think when they see you? Do you want them to end up in a relationship like you had? NO, NO YOU DON'T!" she screamed into the mirror.

Realizing how loud she was, Kelly threw her hands up in front of her face and began crying hysterically into them. There was a soft knock at her bedroom door and Kelly was startled for a moment. Realizing that she must have awoken someone in the house, she regretted her tantrum.

"Mom, mom, are you alright?" asked Rhonda quietly. "I thought I heard you yell."

Kelly could hear the deep concern in her daughter's voice.

"I'm fine sweetie, just upset at myself over my sheer stupidity. I didn't mean to wake you honey. Go back to bed sweetheart, okay?"

"Do you need anything mom?" she sounded as if she were about to cry and that broke Kelly's heart.

"No honey. I'm fine. I'm going to bed now it's been a long night for me. You better head back to bed too okay?" she said trying to hide the pain in her voice.

"Okay, but if you need anything just call me."

"I will sweetie. Goodnight, I love you" she said.

"Goodnight mom. I love you too. I'll see you at breakfast."

"Okay baby. Goodnight."

Kelly could hear her soft footsteps padding away from her door. She looked at herself once more in the mirror. I hope you have enough makeup to cover all of this she thought to herself, and stepped away toward her bed. Kelly stopped midstream and turned around toward her bathroom. She walked up to the sink and turned on the hot water and placed her hand under the faucet waiting for it to warm up. When it did, she turned on the cold water and adjusted it to the temperature that she wanted so she could wash her face. It wouldn't take the redness and swelling from crying away, but it would make her feel better.

Grabbing her towel she walked toward the bathroom door and began drying her face very gently as she entered back into her bedroom. She tossed the towel on the chair at the foot of her bed and climbed back in. This was going to be a long uncomfortable night she thought to herself or morning rather. Glancing at the clock as she tried to ease herself gently under the sheets, she couldn't help but notice it was already almost five a.m. and she would have to be up soon with the girls. Kelly didn't believe that sleep would ever come considering how much pain she was in. However, she was also exhausted from the stress, anxiety, and crying. Sleep overcame her, but it didn't last long.

CHAPTER TEN

It was seven a.m. when Kelly awoke to a sudden burst of pain. She accidentally rolled on to her side in her sleep and it felt like the pain renewed itself. The thought of trying to get up disheartened her. Her mind was having flashbacks of its own accord.

Placing her hands on either side of her head and grasping her ears Kelly thought to herself that she had to stop doing this. The pain of lifting her right arm was immense. Get yourself a cup of coffee and some clothes on so you can do what you were told to do today.

Her sleep deprived brain was slow in functioning. Kelly grabbed her bathrobe off the wall hook beside her bed and put it on. She let out a cry as a surge of sudden sharp pain overtook her movements.

"Kell? Are you okay honey? Do you need some help?" Ryan called to her from the other side of her bedroom door.

"I'll be alright. Just give me a minute to get my bathrobe on" she said, trying to hide the pain in her voice.

"Kelly, what happened last night? Are you okay?" he asked. His voice was full of concern for his friend.

Tying her bathrobe together, Kelly walked to her bedroom door and opened it, neglecting to check the mirror first.

"Oh Kelly" Ryan's mouth dropped as he took in the sight before him. "Oh Kelly, what the hell happened to you baby girl? He said bringing his hand up to Kelly's cheek.

Kelly flinched. She didn't mean to, but it was an automatic reflex.

"Kelly, oh man. I'm not going to hurt you sweetie" Ryan said trying to hide the hurt that he was sure was showing on his face.

"I'm so sorry Ryan" Kelly said beginning to cry. "I didn't mean to, I just couldn't help it" and the threatening tears overflowed. She was embarrassed to be seen like this.

"If I ever see that" but Kelly broke off his sentence holding up her hand and shaking her head back and forth. She clearly didn't want to go there right now. There was a lot more she was going to have to deal with starting with an explanation to her children. After that, she would have to file the protective order and criminal charges.

Kelly began walking up the hall toward the kitchen and Ryan couldn't help but notice that she could barely do it. He tried to put his arm around her to help her steady herself but she jumped. She was clearly afraid of him and in pain. How Ryan wished he could have five minutes with Eric, but it wouldn't end up good for either of them.

"Wait here a second Kell let me get Rita to help you. I think you would feel a lot more comfortable" he said as he walked past her toward the kitchen.

"Thank you Ryan" she said, but it was barely audible.

Rita could not hide the shock of seeing Kelly's face or the tears in her eyes. "My poor girl" she cried. "What did he do to you?"

"I'll tell you later" Kelly replied. "I need some coffee and a ride to the court house this morning."

"Ryan and I will be happy to take you" Rita said through her tears.

"NO!" It came out harsher than Kelly had meant it to. "No" she said in a softer tone, "just you."

Rita placed her arm around Kelly's waist and proceeded to help her up the hallway. "Whatever you want Kelly, that's fine with me" she told her.

"Thanks Rita. I just can't be around any men right now. The Trooper brought me home last night and I was fine with that, but this morning, I just can't do it." Kelly tried to blink away her tears, not wanting her girls to notice them. She wanted them to believe that this was from an accident, not Eric.

Kelly stepped into the kitchen with Rita still holding on to her so she could walk. Why did she have to feel this way? She thought to herself.

Rhonda was home from school, as they all were because of the flooding and helping her sisters with their breakfasts. After a sleepless night worrying about her mother, she couldn't get herself up to go to school, nor did she want to if it had been open.

"Oh mother" Rhonda exclaimed! "What in the hell did that son of a bitch do to you?" she cried.

With that all of her sisters turned toward their mother and gasped at the sight of her. She looked hideous but none of them wanted to say that. They left their seats at the kitchen table and ran to their mother putting their arms around her. They had tears in their eyes and were all trying to speak at once.

Kelly winced from the immense pain she felt as her children wrapped her arms around her. She didn't want to, but it was an automatic reflex to step backwards away from the pain.

"Slow down girls" Kelly said as she winced in more pain. "I can't understand you when you all talk at the same time. "You first Sarah, then Lily, and then Star" she told them.

"I was so worried about you when you didn't come home when you said. I was so scared that you were in an accident because of the flood. What happened to you mommy?" she cried.

"Yes mom," said Lily. "What happened to you? Did he do that to you and tell the truth!" Lily demanded.

"I don't ever want to see daddy again" wailed Star. "He's a monster" she said as she began to wale.

"I'm okay"

"No you aren't" snapped Rhonda. "Don't lie and cover this up for him like you always do." Rhonda could not keep the edge out of her voice and regretted that. "We all deserve the truth."

"Yes, you do. I'm sorry. I am so, so sorry. I should have known better and you all deserve better than this. Why don't you all sit down and eat your breakfast and I will tell you what happened in a minute. I really need to use the bathroom first" she said turning toward the kitchen bath. "Would someone please make me a cup of coffee?" she asked over her shoulder.

"I will" said Rhonda and she went to the coffee pot to pour some for her mother.

When Kelly came out of the bathroom, she sat at the table where Rhonda had set her coffee. She could smell the Irish Cream coffee creamer and it was a treat to her still slightly swollen nostrils.

"Where do I begin?" The question was directed more to herself than to anyone else.

"Try the beginning" said Rhonda. "We need to know what happened to you."

Kelly nodded her head and took a sip of the steaming liquid. She was stalling to get her thoughts and nerves to cooperate. As she looked off in the distance she wrung her hands nervously and looked at everyone gathered around the table with her. She knew they deserved an answer, an explanation, but she wasn't sure she could really give them the whole truth.

"Last night I went to see Eric like he asked me too" she began looking at each of them as she spoke. "When I got there, things were not what I expected" she was trying hard to stay in control of her emotions. "As I walked up the house, I could smell trash burning. I thought that he must be burning his trash and I walked up to the door and knocked. After he

71

answered the door and let me inside, he locked the door behind me. I could see the fire blazing through the living room window."

Kelly picked up her coffee and took another sip. All eyes were on her and she could tell they were hanging on her every word. Her hands had a slight tremor and she was struggling hard to maintain her emotions.

"He went to the sofa and was emptying the ashtray in the trashcan and picking the butts back up and throwing away everything in his wallet and putting it back." There was no sense giving them all the details she thought.

"I told him I could leave and come back another day and he wasn't happy with that." She picked up her left hand and swept her hair away from her face. "He asked me if I was coming back and he basically didn't like my answer. I could see a fire burning in the back yard and asked him if he were burning trash and he told me no. He said it was my clothes."

"No he didn't" Rita said with anger. Her eyes were filled with fury and if Kelly didn't know better she would have expected to see fire shooting from them.

"That's when I noticed he had barricaded all the doors and windows except for the one behind the couch. I knew then that I walked into a trap and I wasn't going to escape. I knew when he looked at me that I would not be able to reason with him." Tears were threatening to fall but Kelly would not allow that in front of her children.

"He had told me I still had some things there and he wanted me to get them. However, when I picked up one of my bags he flipped out. He started ranting and raving about his stuff was in it. I told him there was nothing of his in my bag. He then accused me of stealing his things. It got pretty ugly after that and I don't wish to talk about it right now in present company. It isn't suitable for young ears."

"Who has young ears mommy?" asked Star. She had tears running down her sweet little face and looked as though she had the weight of the world on her little shoulders. It broke Kelly's heart to see her this way.

"We all do" she said wiping Star's teary eyes with her left hand. "I need to get going gang. We can finish this conversation this afternoon when I get back. Rita, will you drive me to the court house? I have to file some papers with the commissioner and the court."

"Of course I will. Ryan, take care of the kids for us okay?" Rita asked apologetically.

"Of course I will. That goes without saying. Be careful you two" he said as he hugged Star to keep her from crying and running after her mother. "Star and I will make dinner for you."

"Can we make a cake too Uncle Ryan?" she asked with tears brimming her eyes.

"Of course we can. But you have to mix it because Uncle Ryan doesn't know how to do that stuff" he told her as he winked at Rita and Kelly.

"Bye mommy."

"Bye baby girl. I'll be back soon, I promise."

"Okay. I'll watch Uncle Ryan and my sisters and keep them out of trouble for you." Everyone laughed. Kelly winced in pain and hoped that no one noticed. She grabbed a jacket and her purse and walked out the door in front of Rita and got in Rita's car.

Rita got in the driver's seat and looked at Kelly. "What is it you're not telling me?" she asked pointedly.

"I didn't want to ride in my car. I don't think I can lift my arm to shift today."

"That's not what I'm talking about and you know it Kelly Price!"

"He beat me Rita. He literally was going to kill me last night. It was only by the grace of God that I made it out alive. He had every window boarded up and all the doors too." Kelly began crying hysterically.

"It's okay Kell. You're home with us and I promise we will never let him near you again." Rita reached over and patted her best friend's knee. "I wish I could do a magic fix for you sweetheart, but I can't. You need to open up and tell me what happened to you."

"I just can't right now" she said wiping her eyes and then blowing her nose. "Please, just take me to the court house."

"We're as good as there" Rita told her and put the car in reverse.

CHAPTER ELEVEN

Rita pulled the car into the courthouse parking lot. The ride had been silent and an uneasy feeling filled the air. Kelly nerves were battling it out within her. She was torn between loyalty to her husband and having him arrested for trying to kill her. She looked at Rita with shame, guilt and fear in her eyes. Rita reached across the seat and grabbed Kelly's hand.

"It's going to be alright. I'm here with you Kelly. You're doing the right thing, you need to know that."

"Are you sure Rita? I mean, are you really sure? This could end up being the thing that sends him completely over the edge. I could end up dead after this." Kelly was beginning to cry as her mind raced with every bad thought imaginable.

"Kell, you are going to be fine. We will be there for you, but this isn't just for you. It's for the kids too. Kell, if you don't put an end to this he's going to end up killing you anyway, then what? Your kids grow up without their mother? Get a hold of yourself damn it!"

"You don't think I've thought about that? Damn it Rita it's all I've been thinking about, but he's my husband. I made a vow before God in church. How do I just abandon my commitment?"

"Oh and you think that God wants you to live like this? No Kelly, He doesn't. Now get off your ass, get in here and file those charges and that protective order." Rita's eyes were burning with angry tears. Tears for the anger she felt toward the man that was still destroying her best friend. When will his hold on her ever end? Rita thought to herself.

"I know you're right" Kelly replied dabbing her eyes with a tissue. "Let's go before I start thinking too much again and change my mind. I don't want to live this way and the only way it's ever going to stop is if I put a stop to it. This is step one and I guess step two" she said smiling weakly through her tears.

"That's right! Now come on sweetie, let's go in and talk to the commissioner."

They both stepped out of the car and began walking toward the back of the courthouse where the commissioner's office was located. Rita hooked her arm in Kelly's and smiled at her as she helped her walk across the parking lot.

"You're really doing the right thing" she told her as they walked.

"I know" Kelly replied halfheartedly.

When they reached the door, Rita rang the buzzer.

"Yes? Who is it and what can I do for you?" a strong male voice asked.

"My name is Kelly Price. I was sent here by Trooper Fielder to file assault charges against my husband and a protective order."

A buzzer rang and the door clicked. Rita grabbed the handle and pulled it open, stepping aside so Kelly could enter first. They could see a gray haired gentleman through the glass pane on the first door to their right and he was motioning them inside.

He could not completely hide the shock on his face when he saw Kelly. "My name is Commissioner Smythe" he began, "please have a seat" he said motioning for them to sit in the chairs behind them. "What can I do for you Mrs. Price?" He asked looking at Kelly.

"Trooper Fielder told me I needed to come in here this morning to file charges against my husband with you." The bruises on her face were even darker than they had been at breakfast and the stitches she had really stood out against the blue.

"I need you tell me everything that happened and when" he said looking directly into her eyes.

"My husband invited me over last night" she began when the commissioner held up a hand and spoke.

"Am I to understand that the two of you don't live together?"

"That is correct sir," Kelly replied.

"Are you legally separated?" he asked

"No, we had had a problem several months earlier where he had locked himself in one of our daughter's bedroom and began using drugs in front of her. He had become violent that night when I tried to stop him and called my best friend here," she said pointing to Rita with her left thumb "and told her either she picked us up or he was going to kill me." Kelly was fighting back the tears that were threatening to fall.

"So, let me understand. He threatened to kill you once before and was using drugs in front of your children and you went back to see him?" Kelly must have looked horrified, for the commissioner quickly added "I'm not passing judgment on you Mrs. Price, I just need to understand what happened."

"I understand she said," dabbing her tears with a tissue from his desk. "He had told me he was attending drug classes and was going to anger management. He said he had stopped drinking and was changing. He told me that he wanted to see the kids and make them a pizza and they had never had closure, so I thought that I would let them eat lunch with him and say their final goodbye. I never had any intention of going back to him." She was openly crying now and the commissioner was doing his best along with Rita to console her.

"Mrs. Price, I know this is hard for you. He is a monster, any man that can do something like this to a woman is not a real man" he said in disgust. "Please Mrs. Price, try to go on. I need to know everything so I know what all I can charge him with. Didn't the trooper go to your house?" he asked.

"No sir, he couldn't. It was flooded and no one could get through."

"Please go on with what you were telling me" his voice was much softer now. He could not stand the fear in this woman's voice and in her eyes. "Did he expect that you were going to reconcile your relationship?"

"No, he couldn't have. After the kids had had lunch and it was time for us to go, he asked me if I would come back" her heart rate was beginning to race. "He asked if I would come back home and I said I didn't think I could do that now. He said we could talk about what I wanted, like if I had wanted a divorce. That's why I agreed to go. I wanted to talk about the divorce. I thought we could handle it like two adults." Kelly wept hard. She was choking as she spoke and beginning to sob.

"Calm down Mrs. Price. He isn't here and he cannot touch you here." The commissioner was shaking his head back and forth with disgust and distaste for this man. He loathed the man that could harm this woman the way he did, and encouraged Kelly to keep talking. "I need to know every detail, however horrifying that may be."

"When I got there, I could smell smoke. It was very pungent. Eric opened the door and I walked inside. He ushered me toward the living room. I saw the fire burning through the back window of the living room. Eric asked me if I was going to come back and I told him I had already told him no. I said I didn't want to live there and he said he" Kelly began sobbing uncontrollably. "He said, maybe you don't need to live" she choked the words out. "I knew right then he was going to kill me."

Rita squeezed her hand and looked helplessly at the commissioner as if to say "hasn't she been through enough?" Kelly looked at Rita for a moment and then back at the commissioner ready to go on telling her horrifying ordeal.

"I said I just wanted to get the rest of my things from the bedroom and he said I didn't have anything there. He said it was all out on the burn pile. I said no, no, you didn't and he told me that I still had a few things there and that I could get those and leave. I walked back to the bedroom and he came up behind me kissing my neck and trying to convince me that I wanted to have sex with him. He told me that if I told him that I really didn't want to, I could get my things and go." The tears were still overflowing and Kelly was going through tissues as if she had stock in the company.

"I picked up my beach bag and that's when he lost it. He said that I couldn't take that. He said he had something in there. I told him it was empty. I handed the bag to him and he looked at it. I tried to get past him but he was blocking the way. He accused me of stealing from him. He then backhanded me with his right hand, lifting me off my feet and sending me into one of the closets. I tried to pick myself up trying to catch my breath. He pulled me up by my hair and punched me in the chest.

"What hand did he use?" asked the commissioner.

"His right hand. He punched me across the bed sending me into the closet. I was having a difficult time breathing. I thought I was going to die and he grabbed me with his right hand and backhanded me again with his left. Then he backhanded me with his right hand again." Kelly was still sobbing as she told of her horrifying ordeal.

"I was trying to get away from him but he grabbed me by my pants. He had caught my belt loop and I heard it snap. He punched me in the back and I thought his fist went straight through me." Kelly put her face in her hands as much to hide her shame as to support her heavy head.

"Is this in the order that things happened?" he asked softly.

"I think so. Everything happened and my mind has been trying to shut it out. I'm so sorry" Kelly sobbed. "I'm trying to remember everything in order."

"It's okay. Is it to the best of your knowledge?" he asked.

"Yes. Yes, of course."

"Please go on then."

"I was trying to get away and he dragged me back by my hair. I was kicking at him trying to get away when I kicked him in the thigh. I was trying to hit his manhood, but I didn't quite connect. I know at some point I had kicked him in the chest, but I don't know when" she was grabbing at the sides of her head trying desperately to remember everything correctly. "I ran to the kitchen and I was screaming for someone to help me. When I got to the kitchen I saw that he had the deadbolt locked on the door. I grabbed the phone to dial 911 and he ripped the cord from the wall. He said he was going to kill me. I remember asking what his father would do if he killed me and he unbolted the door and threw me with all his strength down the stairs. I managed to get in the car before he reached me. I called 911 from my cell phone and met the trooper a few miles up the road because he couldn't get to me." Kelly's eyes were swollen from crying so much and having been beaten.

"Well, I have enough here to charge him with attempted murder, assault, assault with intent, and a few more things. I need you to write down what you just told me and then the charges can be filed. After that, you will need to go upstairs and see one of the ladies at the counter to file for the protective order with the judge. You don't have to write out a long version, just the facts of what he did to you and here is some additional paper if you need it."

"She can't do that here? File for the protective order I mean?" asked Rita.

"No, as long as court is in session it needs to be done in the courthouse. Fill this out for me being careful to write the page number on each page along with your name for each continuing page."

"Thank you, Kelly said taking the paper from him.

"You can fill it out in the room next door and bring it back to me as soon as you're finished."

"I will" she said simply still sobbing though her tears had somewhat subsided and walked out of the room with Rita on her heels.

Kelly filled out the paperwork that the commissioner had given her and read it over again to be sure she didn't miss anything. She stood with Rita's help and began tapping the papers on the table to be sure that they were together and headed to the door.

Rita helped her walk up and opened the door for her and then opened the door to the commissioner's office for her as well. He smiled up at them and motioned for them to sit back down. He made some copies and had Kelly raise her right hand and swear an oath that everything was the truth to the best of her knowledge. After saying it was, Kelly was handed a pen and he showed her where to sign the papers. After that, he handed a copy to her and said that a sheriff's deputy would be in to serve the warrant for her husband's arrest.

"If you have any problems, you dial 911 immediately. Do not wait. I don't care if it's just a strange noise, that's what they're paid for." He looked angry and then said "Men like that should be locked away for good. I hope you feel better soon Mrs. Price."

"Thank you" she replied.

"Now make sure you go upstairs and file for that protective order."

"I'm going to walk her up there now" Rita said and grabbed the door for Kelly and walked her out.

Once upstairs at the courthouse, Rita walked Kelly over to the front desk and told the lady that her friend had been sent up by the commissioner to file for a protective order. The lady winced when she saw Kelly's face and the deep bruises that were on what was showing of her chest.

"Fill this out as best you can and we will give them to the judge. He will then call you to give testimony of what happened and if he finds cause, will grant you the order."

"Thank you" Kelly said accepting the papers from the lady. She walked to another part of the counter and filled out the paperwork. Fifteen minutes later she was handing the paperwork back and listening to the new instructions given to her.

The bailiff showed her in to the courtroom and told her the judge would call her when her case came up.

CHAPTER TWELVE

Kelly and Rita sat in the courtroom together waiting for Kelly's case to be called. "Kelly Price." Kelly jumped at the sound of her name being called. She stood up and said "that's me Your Honor."

"Please step forward and you will be sworn in."

"Thank you, Your Honor" she said as she walked toward the front of the courtroom and the judge pointed to a desk and told her to stand as she was being sworn. After she had been sworn in she was told to be seated.

Kelly took her seat as the judge spoke to her. "I see you have filed for a protective order against an Eric Price. Is this correct?"

"Yes sir Your Honor."

"Please tell me in your own words what happened."

"My husband wanted me to come over and talk about getting a divorce and when I didn't say what he wanted to hear he beat me. He backhanded me into a closet using his right hand and picked me up by my hair. He then punched me in the chest and backhanded me across the bed into another closet with his left hand. He came over to where I landed and backhanded me again. I was trying to get away from him and I started kicking." Kelly began to cry. "He pulled me back by my pants and punched me in the back. I got away and was trying to get to the kitchen to call 911 and he ripped the phone cord from the wall" Kelly sobbed. She was trying hard to control herself but couldn't.

"It's okay Mrs. Price. Do you need a tissue or some water?"

Kelly shook her head no.

"I see that you asked for emergency family support in the amount of five hundred dollars a week. Is that correct?"

"Yes Your Honor. I cannot work at this time and the doctor at the hospital told me it could take as long as a year. I won't have any income and I still need to support our children."

"I see you are also asking for protection for your four minor children as well. That he is not to go to their school, contact them by mail or by phone or by any other means?"

"Yes Your Honor."

I find that there is enough here to find in favor of your request. I need you to fully understand that this a temporary protective order. This order will only last for seven days. He must be served with this order before we can place a full order. Do you understand this?"

"No, why can't you order him to stay away now? He will kill me after this" she sobbed.

"He has to be able to come in and tell his side. I wish I could just take your word for it, but I cannot do that. Can you be here one week from today on Monday at nine am?"

Kelly looked back at Rita who was shaking her head yes. "Yes Your Honor, I can be here."

"Good. We will set this hearing for Monday March thirtieth at nine a.m. and please bring all the evidence you may have relating to this case including any photos or witnesses."

"Do you mean my medical records Your Honor? Kelly asked shakily.

"I mean any and all records you have pertaining to this order medical records, police records, and anything else that pertains to this. Did you file charges against Mr. Price?" he asked.

"Yes I did, before I came here."

"Did you include his current address and phone number?"

"Yes Your Honor."

"Good. We will see you here next Monday for the final protective hearing."

"Thank you Your Honor" Kelly said as she stood up and walked toward the back of the courtroom.

"Mrs Price, if you have any problems whatsoever, please dial 911 immediately."

"I will Sir and thank you."

Rita got up from the bench she was seated on and helped Kelly the rest of the way down the aisle. The bailiff opened the door for them and told Kelly he hoped she healed quickly. Kelly's eyes filled with tears as she said thank you finding it difficult to breathe.

"Let's get you home so you can rest."

"I have a few prescriptions to fill before we do."

"Okay then sweetie, it's off to the drug store we go. After we get your prescriptions filled, we're getting you home to rest. Do we have a deal?"

Kelly tried to draw in a deep breath as she answered, but found it profoundly difficult. "You're right Rita. I really do need some rest. I feel like crap. And I'm having difficulty breathing."

"You poor baby, I don't know how he could have done this to you. I do know that it's over and we won't let him near you again." She squeezed her friend's hand and asked "Do you need anything while we're waiting?"

"Yeah, I do. I need some cokes and some sprite and I would like to grab some milk, teabags, cereal and bread."

"You got it. You sit at the pharmacy while I walk around and pick it all up." Rita walked with her arm around her best friend. Her mind filled with a million thoughts that she knew she couldn't share with her. She wore the brightest smile she could muster so as not to worry her friend.

"You really are the best friend I could ever have Rita. I don't know what I would have ever done without you."

"And you will never have to" she replied smiling.

Rita helped Kelly into the passenger's side of the car and then slipped behind the wheel. She started the car and looked both ways before backing out of the parking space.

"Which drug store are we heading to my dear?" Rita asked brightly.

"I always use the one at the grocery store. They have a complete record of my allergies and they know if any new medications I get will interfere with what I'm allowed to have." Kelly was shaking. She was nervous, afraid, and unsure of what the future would hold. Terrified of how Eric would react once he was charged and then served with the protective order. She couldn't help but think of how he would react after they arrested him. Would they arrest him? Would they just serve him papers and let him go? Would they let her know when he was served?

Her life was seemingly out of control and she felt a desperate need to run but knew she couldn't. She was trying so hard to keep her thoughts under control. Was it normal to have these fears? Her train of thought was interrupted when she heard Rita's voice but couldn't register what she had said.

"Earth to Kelly, are you here?" she said with a slight laugh.

"I'm sorry Rita my mind was a million miles away. What did you say?"

"I said we're here and asked if you could write down a list of what you needed so I could shop while you wait for your prescriptions." Rita looked at her friend with compassion and love. It broke her heart to know that there was something going on with her that she was not telling.

"Sure" Kelly said trying to smile as she reached in her purse and pulled out a pen and an empty envelope. She turned the envelope over and began writing her list on the back. When she was finished, she handed the list to Rita.

"Bread, milk, coke, sprite, cereal, bread, cupcakes, teabags, sugar and evaporated milk, got it" Rita said smiling. "Get your prescriptions out and we'll give them to the pharmacist and you can sit at the pharmacy while I get what you need. Are you sure you don't need anything else?" Rita asked brightly.

"No, I'm going to phone in an order for pizza later and have that for dinner."

"You sure you don't want to get a few of the ones they make here? They're really good."

"You know Rita that might be a better idea. Go ahead and get those. Get two cheese pizzas a pepperoni and one with everything. That way there is something for everyone and there should be some left over."

They walked back to the pharmacy slowly. Rita helped Kelly walk up to the counter and Joe the pharmacist looked at Kelly with his mouth hanging open.

"What happened to you Kelly? Were you in an accident? Are you alright?" he asked with genuine concern.

"Confrontation with Eric Joe" Kelly said weakly. "He won."

"No doubt, Kelly did they arrest him?"

"No, they couldn't get out to me when I called and so I had to drive to meet them. The roads were flooded. Since they couldn't drive to the house they couldn't arrest him. I had to file charges against him and file for a protective order."

"Please tell me that they will put him under the jailhouse. No man should ever put his hands on a woman. I have a few choice other words I'd like to say, but they really aren't fit for you to hear."

"Thank you Joe" she said as she handed him her prescriptions. He took them gently from her hand and looked at each one carefully.

"I can have these ready for you in about fifteen minutes. Why don't you have a seat right over there while I fill them" he said pointing at an unoccupied blue vinyl chair in the corner.

"I think I will" Kelly said as Rita guided her toward the chair. After helping Kelly in the seat Rita took the list that Kelly had written and told her she would be back in a few minutes.

"Will you be okay until I return?" asked Rita

Kelly was terrified at the thought of being left alone and she didn't know why. "Yes" she said lying as much to herself as to her best friend.

"Of course she will" said Joe. "I will be right here to look after her. I won't let anything happen to you Kelly" Joe told her noticing the terror on her face. "I promise."

"Thanks Joe" Rita said and then turned to Kelly and said "I should only be a few minutes."

Kelly sunk her fingers into the arm of the chair squeezing tightly. Her thoughts were running about a million a minute as she watched her friend walk away. Joe tried to keep her mind occupied with conversation and a few jokes but Kelly just couldn't stay focused. For some reason being here with Joe was terrifying her, and she couldn't understand why.

"Kelly, did they give you the number to someone you could talk to about this?" Joe asked her with concern.

"Yes they did Joe. A number for the Victims of Domestic Violence hotline." Kelly could feel tears burning the backs of her eyes but refused to let them fall.

"Have you called them yet?"

"No Joe, this just happened last night and I just left the hospital early this morning."

"Do me a favor, call them as soon as you get home okay? They have a lot of programs that can help you."

"I don't want to be one of those women" Kelly said beginning to cry.

"One of what women Kelly?" Joe asked gently. "One of the women whom undeservingly get beat up by their husband?"

"One of those women everyone feels sorry for. One of those women everyone stares at as they walk past. Putting up with people making up scenarios of what happened because they are too afraid to ask." The tears that were once held back fell freely.

Joe grabbed a box of tissues and handed them to Kelly.

"Honey, you have nothing to be ashamed of and not seeking help will not make things better." He was trying desperately to console her and make her understand that getting help would not make people look down on her. "You know the most tragic part of domestic violence? It's that the people it happens to always blame themselves. They think somehow that if they had done something differently it never would have happened. That's not the case. It isn't the fault of the person this travesty happened to! It is one hundred percent the fault of the person that violated them." Joe was looking at Kelly with deep concern. He wasn't sure if anything he was saying was penetrating the guilt she seemed to feeling.

"I don't know Joe I don't know what to do. I feel like if I had never gone to his house, then this would have never happened. If I had never left him in the first place he would not have been put on the edge like he was."

"Kelly, sweetheart, you know that's not true. He had an insatiable need to punish you. There is nothing that you could have done to prevent this. If you had never left him before I honestly believe that you would have been dead by now." His tones were calm and soothing.

Kelly reached for another tissue and wiped her eyes and then blew her nose. "I just don't know what to believe anymore Joe. I just feel . . . so confused."

"That's completely understandable. I have your prescriptions ready sweetie."

"You never cease to amaze me Joe. I will never understand how you can carry on a full conversation and fill a prescription at the same time."

"I aim to please" he said laughing. "But seriously speaking, I pay full attention to what I am doing while I talk."

"I know you do" Kelly replied. "I trust you implicitly. After all, you are the only one that knows my allergies" Kelly said breaking into complete laughter. She didn't know why she was laughing so hard, just that she couldn't stop and it hurt so bad to do it. The pain was burning and sharp in her chest while she tried to draw in deep breaths.

Rita approached while Kelly's uncontrollable laughter flowed on. "Someone let me in on the joke" Rita said looking back and forth at Kelly and Joe.

Kelly could only wipe at the tears falling from her eyes and continue laughing. Joe looked from Kelly to Rita and back to Kelly again. "It's not really what's so funny as pent up anxiety being released. Rita, please make sure she calls the domestic violence hotline number that she was given."

"Um sure Joe. Do you think it's really necessary?"

"Absolutely" he replied. "They will help with counseling she needs as well as a lawyer."

Kelly's laughter suddenly subsided and they both turned their eyes toward her. She was wiping her eyes on what almost seemed like non-stop tears. "She has a real need for it" Joe said in a low whisper. "Please be sure to contact them. She has a long road to recovery ahead of her."

"I promise" Rita said and turned to Kelly. "Kelly I have everything you needed and it's already loaded in the car. How about we pay for your prescriptions and get you home and in bed?"

Kelly nodded her head up and down as Rita helped her out of the chair. Joe and Rita couldn't help but notice how dark the bruises were on her chest. Joe kept thinking how someone ought to kill that maniac and Rita could only think how her best friend didn't deserve this.

Kelly accepted her bag from Joe and slid her credit card and punched the button and signed her name in the electronic box. Joe handed her a receipt and patted her hand. Kelly tried to smile at him but it was a rather weak attempt.

"I hope you feel better Kelly. I know you have given me a whole new appreciation for your friendship and for my wife" he said with a wink and a smile. "You get some rest kiddo Okay? Rita, make her a hot bath to soothe her muscles but don't leave her in it for too long by herself. She should not be standing in a shower."

"I'll make sure that she does Joe. Tell your wife and the kids we said hi. See you later."

Rita helped Kelly walk to the car and get seated inside. Once they had gotten home, Rita ran another bath for Kelly. She couldn't help but think that her friend needed to relax and that a hot bath would help soothe her battered body like Joe suggested.

Rita helped Kelly bathe and then helped her to dry off and get into a button front nightshirt. She turned the bed down and helped Kelly to settle into it. After tucking her in,

Rita went to the kitchen and got a bottle of water and the pills from the pharmacy. She walked everything back to the bedroom to Kelly and handed her the water.

"Which one do you want to take first?" Rita asked taking the pill bottles from the bag.

"None" Kelly replied. "I don't want to take any. I want to have my wits about me if one of the kids needs me."

"Kelly, Ryan and I are here for the kids. They are going to be fine. You need to relax and I can see the pain you're in, it's written all over your face. Take one pain pill or if you're afraid it will make you too drowsy, I'll cut it in half."

"Okay, cut it in half. I am in an immense amount of pain. I don't want them to look at me and see that" Kelly told her reaching her left hand out for the bottle and the pill. She removed one pill and handed the bottle and pill back to Rita.

Rita broke the pill in half and handed it to her. Kelly put it on her tongue and took a deep swallow of the water from the bottle. "Could you get me a glass of ice Rita?" Kelly asked quietly.

"Of course, what time would you like me to put the pizzas on?"

"I guess around four if you don't mind."

"No, not at all" she said walking out the door in the direction of the kitchen.

When she walked in the kitchen, a delicious smell was wafting through the air and Rita had an epiphany. "You and Star made dinner" she said smiling.

"We said we would" he said smiling back. "You said that like you didn't think we would."

"No, I just forgot about that while we were out taking care of things today. Kelly bought some pizzas. I need to get them and the rest of the groceries out of the car."

"We can do that for you Aunt Rita" Rhonda said. "We'll put the pizzas in the freezer."

"Or we can put them in the fridge and eat them for snack later" said Lily excitedly.

"No, we can have them for dinner tomorrow, Star and I made a cake for snack tonight" Uncle Ryan told them.

"That's right! A big chocolate cake just the way mommy likes it" Star chimed in.

"Okay, you guys win" Rhonda told them "we'll eat the pizza tomorrow. Come on Lily. Help me get the groceries out of Aunt Rita's car."

The two girls walked out of the door together. Star looked up at the clock and told her Uncle Ryan that dinner should be ready in an hour. He smiled at her and told her she was getting really good at telling time now.

Rita filled a glass with ice and took it back to Kelly's room. She informed her that Star and Ryan had already begun preparing dinner and that Star had a surprise for dessert. Kelly smiled weakly. The pill was beginning to take affect although not as badly as it would have if she had taken a whole one.

"Tell them thank you Rita. I really appreciate that. I guess I need to make a few phone calls. I need to call my doctor and make an appointment and call that number I was given and find out what I'm supposed to do."

"I guess I'll let you get to doing that. Star is such a sweetheart. All of your girls are. It's so nice the way they all pull together to get the job done no matter what the job is."

"I'm really proud of them Rita. Tell them all I said thank you."

"I will" she said and walked out of the room to give Kelly privacy to make her phone calls.

CHAPTER THIRTEEN

Kelly let Rita know that she had to be in her doctor's office the following morning. She was going to have to have a recheck to make sure she didn't have any problems or complications. She was also going to have to see someone from the domestic violence program. She informed her that the case worker would be at the house around two.

Rita marked everything down and called her employer and informed them that she would not be in to work the rest of the week. She explained the situation with Kelly and was told that that was fine. They wished her friend a speedy recovery and told Rita she could use some of the vacation days she hadn't used last year so she didn't lose her pay. Rita thanked them and told Kelly she was all hers for the week.

Kelly tried to get up to go to dinner, but the pain was excruciating and accompanied by the dizzying effect of the medication. Star and Sarah brought a dinner tray to their mother's room and Sarah went back to the kitchen to get one for her and Star.

"What are you doing?" asked Rhonda.

"Where are you going?" added Lily.

"Mommy can't get out of bed so Star and I made her a tray and it's lonely to eat by yourself, so I made a tray for her and I so that we could eat with her and she wouldn't be alone."

"What a great idea" Uncle Ryan chimed in. "I'll get the folding table and we'll all eat with your mom."

"That's great!" exclaimed Rita. "I'll grab the chairs and Lily you can grab our plates."

"Okay. I'll load up a tray with our plates and a couple glasses of cokes and I'll load a tray for Aunt Rita and Uncle Ryan too."

Excitement filled the air. Ryan brought the table in Kelly's room and Rhonda followed with four of the folding chairs. As Ryan opened the table and wiped it off, Rhonda opened the chairs and positioned them around the table. She then went back to the kitchen and helped Lily carry one of the two trays. Ryan grabbed two more glasses and filled them with ice and coke for Rita and his self and grabbed one extra glass of coke for Kelly. He then carried them back to Kelly's room and set them on the table in front of their plates.

"What is all of this?" Kelly asked smiling.

"We brought dinner to you. Sarah and I are going to eat in bed with you and Uncle Ryan, Aunt Rita, Rhonda and Lily are going to eat at the table. We can watch a movie with you while we all eat dinner."

The smile on her face was priceless. Kelly was so pleased with her daughter's thoughtfulness. She scooted over in the bed and the girls climbed up and settled in beside her. Ryan handed them their trays and drinks and told them not to spill it with a wink.

"We won't silly" said Sarah.

"Look at this fabulous dinner" Kelly said. "We have spaghetti, garlic bread and salad. You even gave me my favorite salad dressing."

"We sure did" Star beamed.

They said their grace and Star found a movie for them all to watch. They had a light conversation while they ate dinner and enjoyed the movie. It was wonderful to Kelly. She had the best kids in the world she thought to herself. When they were finished dinner, Rhonda, Lily and Sarah pitched in together to clean up.

"We can have a special dessert later mommy if you would like some" Star told her mother.

"That sounds terrific. What is it baby girl?"

"I made you a special chocolate cake with Uncle Ryan's help."

"That sounds delicious. I can't wait."

Star walked out of her mommy's room after kissing her cheek and into the kitchen. She saw her Aunt Rita standing at the sink and walked over to talk to her.

"You guys had been gone a long time. Is mommy okay Aunt Rita?" Star asked, her face looking as though she were going to break into tears at any moment.

"She is fine sweetie. She just had a few errands to run and now she needs to rest."

With that Kelly entered the kitchen and all eyes turned toward her. She put her water bottle in the trash and her water glass in the sink.

"You should really be in bed" Rita said pointedly. "Why don't you help her do that?" The question was directed at Star.

"Okay!" she exclaimed with excitement and grabbed her mommy's hand to guide her down the hall.

"Thank you baby girl, I don't know what I would do without you."

"Would you like me to make you some bath water?" she asked her mother with a big smile on her face and feeling so very important.

"That would be wonderful" Kelly told her smiling as brightly as she could. She knew she must look a mess to her children with her swollen eyes from crying and the black and blue marks all over her body. "Yes, that would be a perfectly good idea. I must be the luckiest mom in the whole wide world to have such a beautiful and thoughtful little girl. You made me a wonderful dinner and a chocolate cake for dessert, and now you are going to run me a bath."

Star beamed at her mommy's praises of her. "I'm the lucky one mommy, I have you." Star's smile could have lit up the world. She walked her mother to the bedroom and helped her to sit on the chair. Star then walked into the bathroom and Kelly could hear the water running in the tub. She could hear a slight splash and smiled to herself thinking about little Star adjusting the temperature of her mommy's bathtub water.

"Do you want it hot or warm mommy?" she called.

"Warm will be fine sweetie, thank you."

The water ran for a few minutes and then stopped. Kelly smiled at the thoughtfulness of such a sweet and innocent child whose only concern right now was for the comfort of her mother. "I really am a lucky woman" Kelly thought to herself.

"Your tub is ready mommy." Star walked over to her beaming from ear to ear. She extended her little hand to her mom and helped her out of the chair. "Do you need help getting undressed mommy?" she asked.

"That would be nice" she told her. Kelly winced in pain as she tried to extend her right arm to let Star help pull off her nightshirt. That pain was deeper than it had been before. Kelly was discovering a lot of new pains as time kept moving forward. With each passing minute it seemed one of her body parts ached more than before.

Star closed her eyes and handed her mommy a towel and said "Here mommy, you can hide behind this until you get in the tub." Kelly smiled as she accepted the towel and thanked her daughter for her thoughtfulness.

She smiled at all the bubbles in the bathtub and said "Thank you Star, this was so very thoughtful of you."

"You're welcome mommy" she said smiling brightly as her mommy sunk into the bubbles. "See mommy? No one can see you now."

"You are so right my precious little baby girl. Thank you again for taking such good care of me."

"You're welcome mommy. Do you want me to wash your back for you?"

Kelly picked up her bath sponge and tried to reach behind her and the pain was excruciating. "Yes I would, thank you sweetie" she said splashing some water and soap bubbles on her face so that Star wouldn't notice her tears.

Star picked up the bath sponge and began very gently squeezing water over her mother's back. She had a horrified look on her face that Kelly could not see. She was shocked at the bruises all over her mother's back. "Is this okay?" she asked gently, afraid that she may be injuring her mother further.

"That's fine," she answered softly. The water actually felt good trickling down her back. However, when Star actually put the sponge against Kelly's skin she had to stifle a scream of pain. She winced uncontrollably and Star was startled by the sudden movement.

"I'm sorry mommy" she said beginning to cry. "I didn't mean to hurt you."

"You didn't hurt me baby. Mommy accidently put her toe on the faucet and hurt her toenail." Kelly lied to her daughter trying to spare her feelings. It wasn't her daughter's fault she was in this condition and hadn't that little girl been through enough already? Hadn't she been going out of her way to make her mommy feel special?

Kelly tried to lean back in the tub but the pain was too deep. It wouldn't allow her to enjoy the water and the sweet smelling bubbles.

"After we get you out of here and settled in bed again, I'll bring you a piece of cake. Are you ready for cake mommy or would you like to wait a little while?"

"I think I'll wait a little while sweetie. Mommy is still full from that delicious dinner you made. You are so thoughtful sweetheart."

"That's because I love you" she said. "Do you need a towel mommy?" she asked sweetly.

"Yes I do honey. But it may take me a few minutes to get up" Kelly said wincing at the effort and the pain that came along with it.

"I can get Rhonda to help if you want me to."

"I think that would be a great idea" Kelly told her and with that Star was out the door and yelling Rhonda's name.

A few minutes later, Star returned with her oldest sister. "I hear you need a little help" Rhonda said smiling.

"As a matter of fact I do" she told her.

Star grabbed the same towel as she had given her mother before to get into the tub. "Here mommy" she said brightly.

"Thank you dear."

Kelly tried to extend her right arm out to Rhonda to help her get out, but it was to no avail. The excruciatingly sharp pain that hit her wouldn't allow her to extend her right arm. Rhonda had to get close to the tub and put her arms under her mother and lift her. Kelly tried to push herself up with her right arm but it gave out.

"Maybe I had better call someone else to come help too mom" Rhonda said.

"No, we can do it. I'll push myself with my left arm and you lift under my arms again. Star, you get another towel so that Rhonda can dry off when we're done" Kelly told her laughing slightly.

Rhonda counted to three and Kelly pushed herself up as Rhonda lifted and they were successful. Star clapped loudly. The two girls helped their mother dry off and helped her back into her nightshirt. After Kelly was dressed the girls helped her in the bed and tucked her in.

Another hour later and everyone joined Kelly in her room for cake, milk and another movie. It was a wonderful way to spend a night after such a horrifying ordeal. The girls gathered up all the glasses, plates and forks and took them to the kitchen and washed them.

Sleep did not come easy and when Rita came in to check on her, Kelly took a whole pain pill and drifted off into slumber. She would wake up on and off from turning and the pain would come relentlessly. Kelly wished she had never went to meet Eric and wished she would never have to see him again. Unfortunately, she knew that wouldn't be the case.

CHAPTER FOURTEEN

When Kelly finally awoke from her on and off slumber, she discovered that the girls had already gone to school. She didn't know how she managed to fall back to sleep at five thirty and not wake up until eight. Rita asked her if she would like one of her pills and she declined.

"No I have to go to the doctor today. I can't afford to go their feeling all out of it. Those pills really messed with me last night. I would drift off and then if I turned, the pain would have me back up. I don't know what to do. I can't take it."

Rita could hear in Kelly's voice just how upset she really was. She handed her friend a cup of coffee with her favorite vanilla creamer. "Would you like a piece of Star's cake for breakfast?" Rita asked her.

"No thank you. I don't feel much like eating today. I need to get dressed, brush my teeth and hair and get my butt moving."

"Do you need some help?" asked Rita.

"It would probably help me a lot" she tried to say with a laugh, but her body didn't appreciate the humor.

"Let's get you dressed" Rita told her and led her down the hall to her room. "What do you want to wear?"

"Something that's easy to pull on and take back off" she replied with a smile. "The shirt has to be a button front though because I can't lift my arm for a pullover."

"You've got it sweetie. How about that dark green blouse and leggings?"

"That will be fine. That blouse is long enough to cover my butt in those" she said laughing and then winced from the pain caused from the effort it took.

"You know, you should really stop trying to humor yourself," Rita told her. "You're only making matters worse."

"He took everything from me Rita. I can't let him have humor too." The look in Kelly's eyes was so sad that Rita felt bad for what she had just said.

"I didn't mean you can't laugh sweetie. I meant that you shouldn't. It puts you in so much pain."

"I know, but if I don't laugh, or at least try to, he wins this too."

"I understand completely" she told her and then helped her into her clothes.

Kelly then walked into her bathroom and got her toothbrush out of the holder, ran some water over it and applied some toothpaste. She looked in the mirror hard at herself. She gazed over the stitches and thought about how much it was going to hurt to brush her teeth. She opened her mouth as wide as she could which was barely half an inch, and began to slowly and carefully brush her teeth. When she finished, she rinsed her mouth with some water and then her antiseptic mouthwash. When the mouthwash passed over her lips, she re-thought that thought. She would not use that mouthwash until she was healed.

Kelly gently patted her mouth dry. She straightened the towel back on the bar and then walked out to the bedroom.

"I'm ready to get more coffee now."

"Good" said Rita. "I need some before we go too."

The two of them left Kelly's bedroom and walked to the kitchen to get their mugs and fill them with the brew that was going to jump start their day. When they walked in the kitchen, Ryan was there sitting at the table.

He looked up and smiled as they came in. "Good morning girls" he said to them winking his right eye. "How are the two most beautiful women in all of the county doing today?"

"In all of the county? Really Ryan? The county?" Rita asked with a mischievous smile on her face.

"Well you usually yell at me if I say the world" he retorted with big laughter.

"I'm afraid I don't fit that remark today" Kelly said trying to smile. "Have you seen my face lately?"

"Yes I have" Ryan told her, "and you are still beautiful to me."

"You can't argue that one Kell" Rita said pointedly. "The black and blue bruises on your face are just making your eyes look even bluer than before. You have that intense ice blue color and when someone looks at them they can't look away."

"Rita, grab my boots please. It's getting really deep in here" she told her laughing and trying not to.

"Hey at least you're in good spirits today" Ryan told her.

"Yes I am. I won't let Eric take that from me."

"Good for you! You shouldn't. Now what have you girls got planned today?" he said, eyes twinkling.

"I am taking Kelly to her doctor's appointment and then we will be coming back here so she can get a phone call she's expecting."

"Well you girls better be careful and Kelly, good luck at the doctor's."

"Thank you Ryan. We shouldn't be too long" Kelly said while slipping into her flip flops.

Kelly then walked to the coffee pot and filled her mug. Rita handed her the vanilla creamer and Ryan handed her a spoon. She thanked them both and told Rita she was ready to go.

Rita gave Ryan a kiss on his lips and told him they would be back in a couple hours. She told him to call her on the cell phone if he needed her. Ryan gave them both a hug, but Kelly's was a light hug because he didn't want to hurt her. Kelly jumped a little when he did but it wasn't just from the pain, it was also out of a strange fear.

Rita and Kelly both grabbed a light jacket and their purses and headed out the door to Rita's car. Once inside, Kelly's nerves began to try to get the best of her. Something must have shown on Kelly's face because Rita asked her if everything was alright.

"I'm just nervous for some reason. I don't know why but I just had a sudden surge of fear."

"I think that's normal considering the circumstances" Rita said to console her.

"I know. I just don't like the feeling" she replied with a halfhearted smile.

Rita patted Kelly's knee and started the car. She put on her seatbelt and looked over at Kelly.

"Want me to help you with yours?"

"No, I don't think I could handle the pain of it touching my shoulder today" she told her friend very pointedly. "I don't mean to sound harsh Rita."

"You're fine sweetie. I understand completely. Maybe you should ask your doctor for an exemption from wearing your seatbelt until your pain lessons."

"That's a brilliant idea Rita! I think I'll do just that." Kelly automatically reached up to her face and gently put her fingers to her lips. "I honestly didn't expect it to hurt so much when I eat or speak" she said.

"Those will be out in a week to ten days. It won't be so bad then" Rita offered.

"I know" Kelly said weakly.

Rita backed the car out of the driveway and they were on their way. They arrived at the doctor's office thirty minutes later. Rita helped Kelly out of the car and into the doctor's office. The receptionist looked at Kelly with sympathy, just the thing she didn't want. "Oh my goodness! Are you okay Kelly?" she asked.

"I honestly don't know."

"How did this happen? Were you in an accident?"

"No, I had a confrontation with Eric" she said.

"I hoped they locked him up!"

"No, not yet" Kelly replied.

"Why on earth not? What the heck is wrong with our system?"

"They said they couldn't arrest him because the roads were flooded and they couldn't get to the house to actually see the situation. I did file charges though and a protective order."

"Do you have the order with you?"

"Yes. Why?"

"I'll need to take a copy and put it in your medical record so that he cannot come near you here, or have access to your medical records. That is unless you want him to have access to your records?"

"Absolutely not" Kelly said reaching in her purse with great effort to retrieve the protective order. "This is only a temporary one. I have to go back to court Monday for a full one."

"When you get the full one" the receptionist said while taking the copy from Kelly "make sure you bring it here so I can put the final order in your records too."

"I will" she said.

"Now, has any information changed since you were here last month?"

"No. Not since my physical. I'm still living at the farm and he still lives at our house."

"Any insurance changes?"

"No."

"Okay. Just sign here on this line to show there are no changes and Doctor Lair will be right with you. You are her first patient of the day."

"Thank you" Kelly said and turned to have a seat in the waiting room.

About fifteen minutes passed and Kelly's name was called to go back. Rita asked if she would like her to accompany her and she said yes.

Kelly went through the doorway and sat in the first chair as she was directed by the nurse. The nurse took her temperature and pulse while asking her what happened. Kelly wished everyone would stop asking these questions but answered anyway. The nurse then took her blood pressure and recorded her weight when she stepped on the scale. Kelly could not believe that she had only gained three pounds since being separated from Eric.

"I see you are finally gaining some weight. That's good but don't get discouraged if you lose some additional weight as a result from your injuries."

Kelly didn't reply, she just followed the nurse down the hall to the exam room with the help of Rita. "The doctor will be in shortly" she said as she slipped the file on the rack on the door and walked out closing the door behind her.

Ten minutes later Doctor Lair came in. "Kelly, I read the report the hospital sent over. Has anything changed?" she asked. "Are you in worse pain or do you have other symptoms?"

"I'm in worse pain with each passing day. It hurts to breathe, I positively cannot take a deep breath and I can't reach out with this arm" Kelly said pointing to her right arm with her left hand. My back hurts horrifically and my face and mouth hurt as well as my neck and the deep pain in my chest."

"Can you tell me what happened?" she asked gently.

Rita squeezed her left hand gently to encourage her to go on. Kelly put her left hand up to her eyes trying not to let the tears of pain and frustration flow. She told the doctor everything she could manage to say. She told her how he punched her in the chest and the blow to her back. How he drug her by her hair and the rest of the terrifying story.

"And they haven't locked him up?"

"Not to my knowledge" Kelly said.

The doctor got her stethoscope and told Kelly that she needed to listen to her lungs and that it may hurt with all her bruising. Kelly tried to prepare herself to no avail. The pain was excruciating. Doctor Lair told her to take a deep breath and Kelly told her she couldn't do that.

"Do the best you can" she said and Kelly complied. Then the doctor examined her head, ears, eyes and mouth. She had Kelly try to bend, but that was not happening. Kelly couldn't even begin to bend the way the doctor wanted her to. She examined Kelly's back, and found profound bruising and swelling between her shoulder blades and on her low back around the sacrum. "I believe you may have a broken sacrum" she told Kelly. "We will need an x-ray of that."

"What is a sacrum?" Kelly asked.

"It's the top portion of the tail bone."

She then had Kelly stretch her arms out in front of her, but Kelly could not raise her right arm. "Squeeze my fingers with your hands" she told Kelly.

Kelly tried to comply but was unable to squeeze with her right hand. She then had her do a few more tests which Kelly failed miserably she thought.

"We know you have an extremely traumatic chest wall injury. You have a broken sternum and a detached rib from the chest wall. What we need to know now, is what is wrong with your right shoulder. I am going to send you for an MRI. Instead of getting the x-ray of the sacrum, I am going to include it on the MRI order."

"What do you think is wrong? How long will I take to heal? I have houses to clean and this is spring cleaning season."

"You won't be doing any work for quite a while. I am writing you out of work for a month, but I need to see you back as soon as we have the results of the MRI. As far as the healing of the chest wall though, that can take anywhere from a year to two or three. You see, every time you breathe, and you have to breathe, you pull the chest apart. As it begins to heal, it also is reinjured. It will be a very slow process."

"Can I do some type of therapy for it?" Kelly asked beginning to panic.

"Absolutely not! Any exercises that you would do in therapy would only aggravate your injury further. This is very delicate Kelly and a woman in your condition and I mean allergy wise, cannot sustain adding insult to injury. You can't afford to aggravate your condition any more than it already is. If you try to exercise it you will be pulling on the chest wall and it won't be able to repair itself. We can't repair it with surgery, you're too allergic to medications" she told her sympathetically.

"So there isn't anything we can do for it?" Kelly asked.

"Not at this time. I need you to get the MRI and then we'll talk after that. Do you have a protective order?"

"I have a temporary one. I have to go next week on Monday to get the final order."

"This work note should help your case and I will give you a copy of today's findings. Make sure you show them to the judge."

"I will" Kelly told her.

"Okay, my office will make your appointment for you. I will see if they can get you in today for the MRI."

"Thank you, I appreciate that."

"I understand that the hospital gave you pain medication. How much did they give you?"

"Enough for two weeks I think" Kelly said.

"Okay, I'll write you another prescription when you come back in."

"Thank you" Kelly said.

"You're welcome. Wait here for a few minutes and my nurse will be back with your MRI appointment and a copy of my notes."

"Thank you DR. Lair" Kelly said her thoughts now racing.

"You're welcome. She'll be right back. Just hold tight" she said and walked out of the door.

In what seemed like hours later but was really only fifteen minutes, the nurse came in with the copy of Kelly's medical record for the visit. She handed her a slip of paper with an MRI referral on it and told her to go straight over to the hospital, they had an opening right now. Kelly thanked her and Rita helped her down from the bed and out the door.

Kelly handed the receptionist her discharge papers and was given a copy of her work excuse. She thanked the receptionist and left for the hospital with Rita. After arriving at the hospital, Kelly checked in and gave them all the pertinent information they needed. She was taken back to radiology and had her MRI about fifteen minutes later. They told her that her doctor would receive a copy of the results in a day or two but she could take a copy of the film with her. Kelly thanked her and said she would like to take a copy. They asked if she wanted the films or a disc and she opted for the films. She thought that she may be able to use them in court and the judge may not have a computer to view the disc.

When she had the films in her hand, she and Rita left the hospital. They stopped at a fast food restaurant and had lunch. Kelly didn't eat much she had a milkshake while Rita had a cheeseburger. They retrieved their food from the drive-thru window and ate on the run.

When Kelly got home Ryan gave her a message that she needed to call the sheriff's office.

"What on earth for?" inquired Rita.

"Apparently it pertains to Eric but they wouldn't give me the information."

"What's the number?" Kelly asked reaching for the phone. Ryan gave it to her and she carefully dialed the number. A voice on the other end of the receiver informed her that she had reached the sheriff's office and asked how she could help her.

Kelly replied that she had a message to call the sheriff's office in connection with her husband Eric Price. The voice on the other end told her to hold.

Another voice came on the line and told her that they were trying to serve Mr. Price with a protective order as well as an arrest warrant for assault. Kelly felt relief flush through her. The voice told her they needed a good address for Mr. Price and Kelly told them his home address.

"We have been unable to locate him their" said the voice.

"You will find him there before six in the morning and after eleven p.m. otherwise you will find him between four and eleven at the bar." Kelly continued talking to the voice on the other end of the line and gave them the name of the bar.

"We will notify you as soon as he is served Mrs. Price. Has he bothered you or tried to contact you since you swore out the protective order?"

"No, I haven't heard from him" Kelly answered honestly.

"Let us know if he does."

"I will" she said and then she thanked him and hung up the phone.

"What was that all about?" Ryan asked her.

"They needed a good address to find Eric or a place he could be found so they could serve him. They told me they would let me know when he was served."

"That was nice of them" said Rita.

"They are required by law to do that" Ryan said irritated.

"What's wrong Ryan? Why are you so upset about that?"

"Because they should automatically be casing his house for him. They should not be calling Kelly and asking her where to find that maggot." Ryan was definitely angry over Kelly's phone conversation. "It's their job to look for him. They know where he lives and they should be checking every couple of hours."

"That's true Ryan, but you never know if they have been and Eric ran. Maybe he left the county so they couldn't get him" Rita said not believing the words that just spilled from her mouth.

Ryan shook his head and said "maybe Rita, but I don't think so" and walked to the refrigerator and grabbed a can of coke.

"I don't care" said Kelly, "just as long as they get him."

Ryan and Rita turned to look at Kelly who was just standing and staring out the window absentmindedly with tears trickling down her cheeks. Ryan walked over to put his arm around her shoulder and Kelly jumped and stifled a scream. "I'm sorry Kell, are you ok?" he asked.

"Yes" was all she said backing away from him with absolute terror written all over her face. Rita ran to Kelly's side motioning for Ryan to leave. "It's alright sweetie, I've got you" Rita told her as she put an arm around Kelly's waist and guided her away from the window and into the living room.

Kelly's walk was slow due to her pain but Rita was patient with her while she walked. "They will get him Kelly" Rita said soothingly.

"I know they will. I'm so sorry about Ryan, I don't know why I jumped. I just felt like I couldn't have him near me" she cried, the tears now streaming down her face. "I'm so sorry."

"You didn't do anything wrong sweetie. Ryan understands. Kelly, you've been through a lot and this will all take time. We need to get you in to see the therapist and to the rest of your appointments. It's going to be a long row to hoe sweetie, but I'm here for the long haul. Okay?" Rita smiled at her hoping it went up to her eyes, but didn't believe it had.

"Okay" was all she said then took a seat on the sofa and just stared out of the window. Rita sat next to her for a moment and then forced herself to get up and walk away before she started crying herself.

Rita was back in the kitchen with Ryan but didn't know what to say. Ryan was pacing back and forth with a worried expression on his face. He rubbed his hands together and then slid his left hand through his thick hair. His brown eyes were somber when he looked at Rita and began speaking.

"I'm really worried about her babe. This isn't the only time she was afraid to be near me. I would love to punch that son of a bitch dead between the eyes for what he did to her. The sparkle is gone from her eyes and she no longer has a bounce in her step. With each passing day she is becoming more and more withdrawn and I think she's afraid of men."

"It will pass honey. She's been through a lot and she just needs a little time. I'll take her in to see that therapist and she'll be okay."

"Don't try to fool yourself Rita. She needs more than therapy I'm telling you this is serious. She needs a psychologist. She needs someone to help her through this thing."

"I know you're right, but I can't think of her that way Ryan, it breaks my heart. I want the old Kelly back."

"I think the kids would like that too don't you babe?"

"Of course, I just keep hoping that in time she will be her old self again."

"And what if she isn't Rita? What then?"

"I don't even want to think like that Ryan. You're standing here talking to me like she's a lost cause right now. She's not a lost cause, I know she'll be okay" Rita said angrily, trying not to raise her voice.

"She will with the right help babe, but not if we all pretend that there is nothing wrong. She needs us to understand and guide her in the right direction." Ryan was good at keeping his temper in check and not letting it show through. Rita on the other hand had a more difficult time with it.

"Ryan!" she exclaimed heatedly "what in the hell do you think I'm trying to do?"

"Do you think this kind of attitude is going to help?"

"No, but it's helping me" she said dabbing at her tears of frustration.

"Why don't we put this conversation on hold for a while okay? Take her to the therapist and see what she says. She may recommend a good psychologist."

"That's a good idea" she said in a calmer voice. "But I refuse to believe she needs a psychologist Ryan" Rita said with anger she was trying to hold back.

CHAPTER FIFTEEN

Rita walked back into the living room and sat down on the sofa beside Kelly. She placed her right hand on Kelly's knee and told her she thought they should make her an appointment to see a therapist.

"Victims of domestic violence as sending someone out here to talk to me 2 o'clock today Rita," Kelly said.

"I forgot about that Kelly. Is there anything you would like me to do before they get here? Would you like me to fix you some lunch? It's almost 1 o'clock."

"Oh my goodness Rita I didn't realize it was that late. I really don't feel like eating anything but I could sure use a glass of Coke or glass of sprite."

"Coming right up, which one would you prefer?"

"I'd prefer the Sprite please."

Rita walked back into the kitchen opened up the cabinet to retrieve a glass and filled it with ice then opened a can of Sprite and poured it into the glass for Kelly. She then walked it back into the living room and handed the glass to Kelly.

"Is there anything you would like me to help you with Kelly?"

"No, I'm good Rita. But perhaps when I'm finish this you can help me back to my room to freshen up and we can get the kitchen ready to receive guests. I really don't want to see anyone in my room or in the living room it really hurts too much this get up and down from the sofa."

"You got it sweetie. I'll be back in about ten minutes to help you back to your room. Would you like me to put on a pot of coffee?"

"That would be great Rita. How about we put the coffee on it about forty five minutes that way it will be fresh when they get here."

"That's fine by me. I'll be back in about ten minutes."

At 2 PM there was a knock at the door. Kelly's company had arrived. Rita opened the door and invited the woman inside saying "hello my name is Rita I believe you're here to see Kelly?"

"As a matter of fact I am. My name is Mrs. Stanton and I'm from the Council for women that are victims of domestic violence. It's nice to meet you."

"It's nice to meet you too," Rita said as she closed the door behind Mrs. Stanton. "Won't you please have a seat while I go and get Kelly?"

"Yes I will thank you," she said as she pulled out a chair from the kitchen table and sat down.

Rita disappeared down the hallway to retrieve Kelly from her room. When she arrived at Kelly's bedroom door she knocked softly and informed her that Mrs. Stanton was there to see her. Kelly thanked her and opened the door and allowed her friend to help her back up the hallway to the kitchen. When Kelly entered the kitchen she offered Mrs. Stanton a cup of coffee.

"Yes that would be nice thank you."

"Do you use cream or sugar or would you prefer a flavored creamer?"

"Just cream please, thank you. If you tell me where it is, I can get it myself."

"The cream is in the refrigerator and the coffee cups are already on the table."

"Do you feel comfortable talking here or is there some other place you would like to go?"

"No, here is fine. I feel so embarrassed and ashamed to have you see me in this condition. I really must apologize for the way I look."

"Please don't apologize. The way you look is not your fault," Mrs. Stanton said as she poured cream into her coffee.

"But it is my fault, if I had never gone to Eric's house this would've never happened. If I had never said anything to him I wouldn't have gotten him so upset."

"Now you're speaking like a typical domestic violence victim. They always believe the fault this their own when it isn't. Your husband had no right in this world to lay a hand on you it is his problem it's his fault not yours not anyone else it's all his!"

The tears were streaming down Kelly's face as she said "I can't help but feel as if I had done something different this would have never happened."

Mrs. Stanton got up from the table walked over to the kitchen counter and retrieved several tissues from a box of Kleenex and handed them to Kelly. She looked Kelly straight in the eye and said "this is not your fault! There is nothing you could have done differently it would have happened eventually. Your husband was a walking time bomb and too many times I have seen the same thing in so many different women. Each believes that it's their fault if they did just differently if they did that differently this wouldn't have happened to them but that's not the case. Men like Eric want to control you they need to have things their way. How many times have you tried to explain your side of the situation to no avail?"

"Almost always, every time something would go wrong it would always be my fault. If a man looked at me it was my fault it didn't matter that Eric was the one that picked out the clothes he would always say I was doing something to entice him meaning the other man." Kelly could no longer hold back the tears that wanted to fall. They were pouring down her cheeks like rain. Mrs. Stanton walked over to the counter and retrieved Kelly some more tissues.

"I just thought that if I went over and talk to him that night that I would be able to explain what was wrong with our marriage that we would be able to settle things between us. That we could close our marriage and still be friends for the children's sake, but that's not how things worked. He became so evil, so violent, so angry it was almost as if I didn't know who he was anymore. I really believe he was going to kill me that night."

"That is such a horrifying ordeal that you had to go through. I'm so sorry this happened to you. Were there any signs leading up to that night that this would happen?" Mrs. Stanton asked as she took her seat back at the table. "Were there any clues no matter how minor that he was unstable?"

"Do you mean that night?" Kelly asked between sobs.

"I mean it any time. Maybe when you first met? Did he ever call you stupid, or tell you what friends you could have, or track you down by yourself and to find out where you are at all times of the day?"

"Yes, Eric did all of those things. He bought me this really nice cell phone and he said it was to keep tabs on me. At first I thought he was joking but the minute I would leave the house he would be on the phone asking where I was what I was doing where I was going how long I planned on being. He eventually started timing me, telling me how long I had to travel to my destination how long he figured that it should take me to be there and do whatever I needed to do be it cleaning someone's house or grocery shopping and how long it would take me to get back home."

"These are the beginning signs of an unstable man. These are the beginnings, are the warning signs of domestic violence. The signs started out subtle, it can be as small as why are you wearing that make up when you go to the grocery store or calling you stupid or calling you other various names, keeping track of your schedule, starting an argument when you don't keep to the time according to their schedule. It can also be with deciding who you can and cannot be friends with. These are all little things, but they are also warning signs. Eventually it graduates to not being allowed to be around family members. Has Eric ever tried to prevent you from being around certain family members or friends?"

"Yes he has, he never really liked me to talk to or go anywhere with Rita. Ryan, well he was totally out of the question. I was never allowed to be near him and we had been friends for about fifteen years. But I was to always entertain his friends." Kelly was sobbing hard and having a difficult time speaking with her sore lip and the excruciating pain emanating from her chest. "If I would go to the store and bring back caffeine free Coke instead of regular Coke he would tell me how stupid I was and how I couldn't follow simple directions."

"I'm so sorry you had to go through that" Mrs. Stanton said. "Unfortunately, you were a victim of domestic violence, in most instances it starts out like that. If you don't know the warning signs then you really honestly don't know the situation you're heading for. I brought along a packet of papers that I will need you to fill out. This will give us permission to hire an attorney for you you're going to need one when you go in for your final protective order. This attorney will make certain that your rights are met and that your husband will not be allowed to influence you."

"I am so scared." Kelly was wringing her hands. She could not sit still, she needed to pace but the more she paced the more pain she was in. "Am I doing the right thing?" Kelly asked.

"You most certainly are!" replied Mrs. Stanton. "You cannot let him get away with this. These men need to be taught a lesson. They need to learn to cherish their wives not abuse them. Now I am going to need to take pictures of all of your bruising if you haven't already done so."

"No, I haven't. Trooper fielder took pictures the night this happened" Kelly cried. "But I haven't taken any of my own."

"Then we need to do that now. This will really help you in court. The judge needs to see the condition that you were in."

"But the judge already saw the condition I was in when I first got the temporary protective order."

"I understand that. But you need to understand that the judge sees thousands of cases. He needs to see the pictures of you when this first happened, it will only help you win your case for your final protective order."

"I understand" Kelly said wiping her eyes and trying to blow her nose. She walked over to retrieve a soda from the refrigerator and pulled out a sprite. She then walked over to the cabinet and retrieved a glass with her left hand, walked over to the refrigerator and filled the glass with ice before pouring the sprite. Kelly took a long drink before setting the glass down on the counter.

"I know this is a lot to take in but honestly it's necessary. You need to learn the warning signs of domestic violence so it doesn't happen again. Also, I need you to know that we have therapists to help you through this emotionally challenging time. Have you found yourself having any difficulties?"

"Like what?" Kelly asked.

"Fears, nightmares just anything that interferes with your normal day-to-day life?"

"You mean aside from the pain?"

"Yes" Mrs. Stanton said softly.

"Yes, I find that I can't be in the same room with any man that resembles the size of Eric, the looks of Eric, oh hell" Kelly said while raking her left hand through her long hair away from her eyes "I can't go to the store and be in the same aisle as a man. I can't even be in the kitchen alone with Ryan."

"I would like you to speak with one of our therapists. I believe having someone to talk to can help you get through this crisis."

"I can't speak to them if they are a man. If you have a female therapist then I can speak with her."

"I understand completely. No one is going to make you do anything that you are not ready to do, we are only here to help you Kelly we're here to help you get through this thing."

"Thank you, I really appreciate everything that you are trying to do for me. But I don't want to be considered one of those women."

"One of what kind of woman Kelly? What kind of woman do you think you are?"

"The kind that everyone looks at in pity, it makes me feel dirty, ashamed and stupid. I don't want everyone to know what happened to me it's my problem."

"No Kelly, it's his problem. He created this mess for you not the other way around. No one is looking at you with pity. They may feel sad for your situation and think "what happened to her" but you don't have to let this bother you. Nothing in this situation is your fault. Do you hear me? NOTHING is your fault. What you are feeling is natural, but it will eventually dissipate."

"I'm having a rather difficult time comprehending or believing that. I can't understand why. Why did this have to happen? Why did this have to happen to me?"

"Bad things happen that are beyond our control. You weren't educated to know what the warning signs were or even thought that it was necessary to be. Now, let me go over this paperwork with you and get this ball rolling. We are running out of time."

Mrs. Stanton opened up the packet of papers and explained thoroughly what each set of papers pertained to and the importance of them. When she explained the last of the paperwork, Kelly began signing what pertained to her situation. When she was finished, Mrs. Stanton went back over the paperwork with her, explaining thoroughly what she signed and why and exactly what it pertained to and what Kelly should expect. She explained to her what to expect at the final protective order hearing as well as what to expect when Eric was arrested and charged for the assault on her.

Mrs. Stanton was in the midst of explaining Kelly's role in the ordeal when the phone rang. Kelly looked at the caller ID but it was a blocked call. Kelly didn't think, she just punched the talk button and said hello. No one was answering, but she could hear someone breathing. Kelly's hand began to tremble.

"What is it?" Mrs. Stanton asked taking the phone from Kelly and putting up to her ear. "Who is this please?" she asked, but the receiver clicked and no one was there. "Do you think this was your husband?" she asked Kelly with concern.

"I don't know" she replied. "There was no one on the other end, just breathing. The call came up blocked."

"Ok, here is what I want you to do. First, get a notebook or a calendar and write down the time, the date and what you saw on the caller ID as well as what you heard on your end of the phone."

"That's just it I didn't hear anything, just breathing for a few seconds. Should I call the police?" Kelly asked terrified.

"They won't be able to do anything, because it was just breathing and a blocked call, but you should call just to log in the fact that this happened and in case it was him and he decides to call back and actually say something."

Kelly called the local Sheriff's office and asked for someone to please come out and log the information. They told her it was not an emergency but would have a deputy out to her as soon as they could. Kelly explained what they said to Mrs. Stanton.

"Would you like me to wait here with you until they get here?"

"No," Kelly said trying not to let her tears fall. "I have no idea when they will get here and I don't want to keep you all day. I'll be alright and besides, Rita and Ryan are here. It may just all be coincidental, right?"

"It may be, but Kelly you really don't want to take chances. Pease be careful!"

"I will Mrs. Stanton and thank you for coming out here and helping me with all of this. I would have never gotten through all of this paperwork or even understood the process without you."

"You're welcome dear. Pease try to get some rest. Remember to log my name down as being here when you received that call."

"I will" Kelly told her and walked over to the door and opened it for Mrs. Stanton.

Mrs. Stanton patted Kelly on her left hand very gently. If you need me, call me. Here is my number. Remember, I am here for you."

Kelly thanked her as she walked out the door and closed it behind the lady whom genuinely seemed to care. But now what was she going to do? Was that phone call a coincidence or was it Eric letting her know that he knows what she did? She was trying not to panic herself but failing desperately. Rita and Ryan walked back into the kitchen and both saw the look on Kelly's face.

"Kelly what's wrong?" they asked in unison.

"Nothing" she replied shaking her head and turning away from them so they could not see the fear in her eyes.

"That was not the look of nothing Kelly Price" said Ryan. I have known you for many years and I know when something is wrong so spill the beans" he told her gently.

"Yes," Rita chimed in. "Tell us what has gotten you upset on top of everything else?"

"Th the phone" Kelly said stammering and pointing toward the phone on the kitchen counter.

"What about the phone?" asked Ryan.

"Nothing really, just me being foolish."

"Nonsense" Rita said as she picked the phone up from the counter and scrolled back the caller ID. "Who called with a blocked call?" she asked gently.

"I bet I know who it was." Ryan said quietly.

"I really don't know who it was. When I answered all they did was breathe into the phone. Mrs. Stanton had me log the call and the Sheriff's office is sending a deputy to take a report just in case."

"Well that reassuring" Ryan said. "When do they propose to get here?"

"Well they told me it wasn't an emergency and they would send someone as soon as they could."

"I see" said Ryan turning his back to Kelly so she would not see his anger. After composing his facial expressions, he turned back to face Kelly again and in doing so saw a patrol car pulling in the driveway. They're here" he said.

"Oh no, I can't let them see me like this" Kelly cried.

"They need to see you like this" Rita reassured her, "so that they take this seriously and understand your situation."

Kelly was not sure that she agreed with her best friend but she didn't have a choice. Like it or not, they were going to see her in this condition.

The deputy knocked on the kitchen door and Rita opened it for him asking him to come in. "I have a complaint that someone here received a prank phone call" he said sternly.

"Thank would be me" Kelly said standing up and turning to face the deputy. The deputy was good at masking his facial expressions, for when he saw Kelly's face he didn't wince a bit.

"How are you ma'am?" he asked with concern. "My name is Deputy Parsons."

"Not good, but trying to heal" Kelly said trying her best to force a smile. "I'm Kelly, Kelly Price."

"What happened? When you received the call I mean."

"I was filling out some paperwork with an advocate from the Victims of Domestic Violence program and the phone rang. I looked at the caller ID and it said blocked call. I answered it and there was no one there, only someone breathing. I handed the phone to Mrs. Stanton, my advocate, and the caller hung up. She advised me to make a report just to have this on record in case it was my husband and anything further happened."

"Do you know if it was your husband?"

"No" Kelly said, "I don't. But I also don't know of anyone else that would call me with a blocked call. I just took a protective order out against him and I'm sure he's angry."

"Why did you take out a protective order on him?" the deputy asked.

"Do you see her face?" Ryan asked astonished.

"Yes sir, I do. But I cannot just make an assumption that the bruises are from him. I need to hear it from her and put that on record. Now back to you ma'am" the deputy said turning toward Kelly.

"A couple of nights ago my husband beat me unmercifully. He said he was going to kill me. I went to the hospital for my injuries and then came home. I was told by Trooper Fielder to file assault charges the following morning and get a protective order."

"Did you do these things ma'am?" he asked.

"Yes I did. Right away, as soon as I was able. I filed the charges and then I went upstairs and filed for the protective order. The final hearing is on Monday" Kelly said, her eyes brimming with tears that were threatening to fall.

"I apologize for upsetting you ma'am, but I really need to hear this for my report, otherwise it looks like someone paranoid over what could have been a wrong number. You are right to call us and make a report. What is your husband's name?"

"Eric. Eric Price" she told him. They charged him with assault, attempted murder, assault with intent and a few other things."

"Yes ma'am, I'm familiar with that name. He has not been picked up yet as far as I know. I was at his home earlier today and he wasn't in. We will pick him up, but in the meantime you need to be careful and you need to keep your doors and windows locked at all times."

"Is that really necessary?" Kelly asked.

"I believe it is. I'm going to write up this report. Here is my card" he said while going in his wallet and retrieving a business card and writing something on the back before handing it to her. "This is the case number. On the front is a number where you can reach me at the station or if I'm not there, you can leave me a message."

"Thank you" Kelly said as she took the card from his hand. "What do I do if he calls back?"

"See if you can get him to say something. If he does and you recognize his voice then we can pick him up for violating a protective order. If he doesn't, then log the call on a calendar or in a notebook. Either way, make sure you log the call. You need to show that this keeps happening and if it does then we can get the phone company to trace the origin of the call."

"Thank you. I'm sorry that you had to come out here for nothing more than a prank phone call."

"I'd rather come out for a prank phone call than have to come for something more serious. Please make sure that you do like I said and lock your doors and windows."

"I will" Kelly told him, "I promise." She put the card next to phone on the counter and opened the kitchen door for the deputy to leave. As he was leaving, the bus was dropping off the two older kids from school. Boy would she have some explaining to do.

CHAPTER SIXTEEN

The girls were full of all kinds of questions when they got in but Uncle Ryan explained to them that the deputy was dropping by to make sure that their mother was alright. He didn't think they needed to know every little detail of what was going on and keeping them in the dark about today's events would keep them from getting even more upset. He asked Rhonda to help her Aunt Rita make tacos for dinner and Rhonda was all for that.

"But what about the pizza mom bought?" Rhonda asked with concern for her mother's feelings.

"I wouldn't be able to eat pizza Rhonda. I probably won't be able to eat tacos either. My doctor called me earlier and told me I should limit my intake to ice cream, milkshakes and Jello." It was a lie, but a little white lie never really hurt anyone did it? She had asked herself. Besides, she definitely could not open her mouth for either of the choices.

"Ok mom" Rhonda said with concern, but I'm making your milkshake at dinner time ok?"

"I would love that" she said wrapping her arms around her daughter's shoulders as best she could in the condition she was in. She could not seem to lift her right arm at all today. The tightening and the pain along with the swelling were worsening. Isn't that the way things went though, things got worse before they got better? She hoped that did not apply in all aspects she was going through today. For if it did, than she could expect much worse out of Eric.

"Mom, why don't you take a nap before dinner? Sarah can run you a bath and you can soak for a little while to relax your muscles and then she can help you into bed. How about it mom?"

"That would be great."

Sarah was beaming at her mother. "Mother, I will make you the best bath you have ever had" she told her laughing.

"I bet you will Sarah, I bet you will" she told her smiling as they walked down the hallway together to Kelly's room. When they reached the door, Sarah helped her to sit on the chair at the foot of the bed. Kelly began unbuttoning her blouse while Sarah went into the bathroom to run her mother's water. She made the water very warm, not hot, but very warm and poured some of her mother's favorite bubble bath in it.

Kelly was struggling with her pants when Sarah came in to get her for the tub. "Let me help you with those mother" Sarah said.

"Thank you, I appreciate the help. I can't seem to move my right arm very well."

I made the water deep mother and I got your inflatable pillow so you can lie back and relax. Maybe the warm water will help ease the swelling and tension in your shoulder. After Kelly and Sarah got her pants off, Kelly walked with her daughter to the bathtub. Sarah turned her head away as her mother removed her underclothes and stepped gingerly into the bath.

"Wow, this feels good" she told Sarah.

"I'm glad that it does" she replied.

As Sarah was leaving the bathroom to give her mother some privacy, the phone rang. Kelly's face went pale. "What's wrong mother? Is the water too hot?" she asked.

"No! Not at all. I just had to adjust myself so I didn't slide under the water" she said with a slight laugh trying to convince her own self that nothing was wrong.

With that, Rita was calling through the bedroom door telling Kelly she had a phone call. She told her it was Trooper Fielder. Kelly blushed but Sarah could not see it for the bruising on her mother's face. Sarah picked up the phone in her mother's room and brought it to her in the bath.

"Trooper Fielder, how are you?" she asked.

"Good thank you, but the question of the day is how are you?" he asked with what sounded like genuine concern.

"I'm good I guess" she said hesitantly. "I'm in a bath now trying to reduce some swelling."

"Oh, I'm sorry. I guess I caught you at a bad time."

"No, no, not at all. It's not as though you can see me." Kelly regretted the words the moment they left her lips. "What is wrong with you?" she asked herself silently. "What can I do for you?" she asked him.

"Nothing, I was calling to see how you are and to make sure that everything is ok. Have you had any problems? Has Mr. Price contacted you?" he asked.

"I think so" she said with hesitation.

"What do you mean 'you think so'?" he asked.

"I mean that someone called here today with a blocked number but all they did was breathe into the receiver. They didn't say anything at all."

"I see. That may or may not have been him. If it was him, then he knows that we are looking for him. Of course it could always be coincidental" he said reassuringly.

"I know it just took me by surprise is all" she said trying to make light of it.

"Did you make out a police report just in case and log the call?"

"Yes, I did. My victims advocate was here and she told me what to do."

"Did you log the fact that there was a witness to the call?"

"Yes I did that too. You sound worried Trooper Fielder." Kelly smiled to herself.

"It's Tom and yes I am. That husband of yours is a dangerous man. I want to be sure that you are alright and don't have any future problems." He was attracted to this woman, he didn't know if it was because he felt sorry for her or if it was because of those piercing blue eyes, but there was an attraction, at least there was for him.

"You don't mind me calling you Tom?"

"Know of course not Mrs. Price."

"Then you have to call me Kelly. I need to thank you."

"Thank me for what?"

"Saving my life! If you hadn't come out to meet me, I might have been dead."

"I just wish I could have gotten to the house, I could have arrested him on the spot. As it is, they still have not apprehended him. I really need you to be careful. Why didn't you call me when you received the prank call?"

"I didn't think it would be right."

"I wrote my personal cell number on the back of my card so you could call me. I don't care how unimportant it may seem to you or how insignificant, I want you to call."

"Thank you Tom for caring."

"Just please make sure you call if anything happens."

"I will, but I just don't feel right doing that. I feel like I'm imposing or being a nuisance."

"You're not a nuisance and you're not imposing." This poor woman, he thought to himself, she is beginning to act like a domestic violence victim, like a battered victim that is afraid of everything they do being wrong. "I gave you my number, please use it."

"I will if anything else arises."

"Good, make sure that you do. By the way, will it offend you if I drop by this evening and check on you and your family? I feel a little uneasy knowing that he is still running free and especially since you received the call. It may be nothing, but I want to make sure your safe."

"Thank you, I would like that very much" Kelly said smiling with difficulty.

"Ok, I'll drop by in a couple of hours then. Keep your doors and windows locked."

How many times was she going to hear that today? "I will and I'll see you in a couple of hours." Kelly hung up the phone with a half-hearted smile on her face. What was she going to do? She is scared to death of men, but not this one. He seems more like a knight in shining armor. Then she thought about her face. What was she going to do about her face? Calm down she told herself. He saw you when this first happened, and he's not coming here for a date she laughed to herself, he's coming to check up on you.

The phone rang again and Kelly answered it without looking at the caller ID thinking that it might be Trooper Fielder again. "Hello" she said happily.

There was no response coming from the other end. "Tom, is that you?" she asked the receiver.

"Who the hell is Tom?" screamed a raging voice. "I knew I couldn't trust you!"

Kelly was horrified! Oh no, what had she done? "He . . . he's the . . ." but her voice broke off choking with tears and fear.

"I knew you were a bitch" the voice screamed at her. "I knew you couldn't be trusted" and the receiver went dead.

Kelly dropped the phone to the bathroom floor and was crying hysterically. Rita came running in the bathroom because Sarah had left Kelly by herself to take a soak and give her the privacy she thought she needed. "What happened Kelly?" she asked grabbing a towel and wrapping it around her.

"The phone" she said pointing to the phone lying on the bathroom floor, her hands shaking.

"What about the phone? Who was it Kelly? Was it Eric?" she asked with extreme concern.

"I don't know. The voice was distorted but he acted like Eric. He said I was a bitch and that I couldn't be trusted. He was screaming at me" Kelly sobbed.

"We need to call the police."

"No, I don't know that it was him" she pleaded. "It sounded like him but I can't be absolutely sure."

"Well tell me about the call" she coaxed her friend.

"I had just gotten a call from Trooper Fielder and he told me to call him Tom before he hung up and the phone rang again as soon as I hung up with him and I thought it was him and I said Tom into the receiver I think. I think I asked if it was Tom."

"It wasn't?"

"No, it wasn't. It sounded and acted like Eric, the voice did, but it was sort of distorted and I couldn't be sure."

"We need to make a report of this like the deputy told you."

"I don't know if I can" Kelly cried.

"Yes you can! Now Kelly, pull yourself together so you don't upset your girls. I know how hard this is for you, but you really need to get this logged. If you don't want to make out a police report then at least call the Trooper."

"Ok, I'll call him but I don't want to look like some sorry desperate can't do a thing for herself woman. I don't want to look like I'm afraid of my own shadow."

"I honestly don't believe that's what he'll think of you." Then speaking in a much softer, gentler tone she added, "I think he will be glad to hear from you, I think he might like you" she said with a wink.

Kelly blushed again under all of the bruising and agreed to call Tom. She let Rita dial the number and when she punched the last number, Kelly accepted the receiver from her.

"This is Tom" said the man on the other end.

"Tom" Kelly said hesitantly, "this is Kelly."

"What's wrong? I can hear from your tone that something's wrong. What happened?"

"After I hung up with you the phone rang again. I thought it was you calling back and I didn't check the caller ID. When

I said 'hello' no one answered. I said 'Tom, is that you?' and a voice started screaming at me about being a bitch and how I couldn't be trusted. It sounded like Eric's voice, but I can't be sure because it was distorted."

"Distorted how?" he asked.

"I don't know. It was drug out or something. He kept screaming at me." Tom could hear how upset she was and he could tell from experience that she was trying to hold back tears. 'Hadn't this woman been through enough at the hands of this monster' he thought to himself.

"It's ok. I'm on my way over. I'm off duty now, but I'll make a report anyway and you can call your local sheriff's office and have them come out and make a report too. I'll be there in about fifteen minutes maybe twenty. Is there anyone there that can stay with you until I arrive?" he asked.

"Rita and Ryan are here with me and the girls" she replied. "They have been staying with us since this happened."

"Good. Let me talk to one of them."

"Ok sure" she said as she handed the phone to Rita saying "he wants to speak to you."

"Hello, this is Rita."

"Hello Rita, this is Trooper Tom Fielder. Can you make sure that Kelly doesn't leave either you or your husband's sight until I get there?" his voice was filled concern and a hint of anger.

"Of course we can. We aren't planning to go anywhere until they catch that jackass."

"Good to hear. I'll be there in fifteen to twenty minutes. In the meantime, make sure that she calls the sheriff's office and makes out another report. It's very important that she does this even if she isn't a hundred percent sure on the voice."

"Ok. I'll have her call as soon as we hang up."

"See you in a few" he said and ended the conversation.

"Your trooper friend wants you to call the sheriff's office" Rita said with a smile. "I think he likes you."

"Rita, this is serious!" Kelly remarked. "He's not coming because he likes me he's coming because he's concerned."

"Keep telling yourself that Kell and you just might believe it. I hear it in his voice. He likes you! Now, call the sheriff's office."

Kelly took the phone from Rita's hand and pulled her bathrobe on with Rita's help. She then walked into the kitchen and picked up the card the deputy gave her a few hours before and dialed the number.

After the voice informed her she had the sheriff's office, she asked for the deputy. "I'm sorry, but he is on duty right now. Can I give you his voice mail or take a message?"

"Yes please. This is Kelly Price. The deputy was just out at my house a few hours ago for a prank phone call from my husband and I believe he just called me again. He was screaming profanities at me and making accusations and I really need to report this incident."

"I will notify him over the radio and someone will be out there as soon as they can. Can you give me your address please?"

Kelly gave the woman on the phone her address and after thanking her, hung up. Now all she could do was wait to see who showed up first and maybe put some clothes on she thought to herself with a smile.

Sarah helped her mother get into her clothes. She helped her with a pair of leggings because she would be able to get those off by herself and a button front blouse. Kelly stepped into a pair of flat sandals because she didn't think she was in any condition to navigate heels nor did she want anyone looking at her as if she were trying to be sexy and failing.

Tom was the first to arrive and Kelly walked him into the living room and told him about the conversation. Rita walked back to Kelly's bedroom to retrieve the phone so Tom could view the caller ID. Kelly looked exhausted and her entire being ached.

Kelly deliberately sat in the darkest side of the room avoiding the lights. "Why are you sitting in the dark Kelly?" Tom asked her gently. "Are you trying to hide the bruises from me? I've seen them before."

"I know you have, but not this dark or profound. But in answer to your question, I'm not hiding from you in the dark . . . it's more like I'm hiding from death. It's just the way I feel now, like I'm hiding from death."

Tom got up and crossed the room to where Kelly was sitting on a love seat by herself. "May I?" he asked motioning toward the cushion next to her.

"Sure" she said sliding over a little more.

"I won't pretend to know how you feel. I can only try to imagine and I don't think that would come close to the reality of it. You don't deserve what has happened to you. But I promise I won't allow any more harm to come to you" he said reassuringly. "You do not have to sit here in the dark and hide from anything. I will always be just a phone call away." Even in the darkened side of the room, this woman that he barely knew looked so vulnerable and defeated that he could not help being drawn to her. There was something about the sadness in her eyes and the desire they had to smile but just couldn't seem to do so.

"I honestly appreciate that" she said simply, "but that's not why I'm here" she said pointing around the darkened side of the living room. "I feel compelled to sit here, to hide to just hide from death." Kelly wiped a tear from her eye before continuing "after my husband and I had our altercation, for lack of a better understanding of what happened, and then these prank calls, I feel as though someone is going to kill me. I don't know why, maybe it's paranoia but that's the way I feel."

Tom reached over and put his hand gently upon Kelly's and she flinched, she didn't mean to it was just a natural reflex from the ordeal she had just been through. "I'm sorry" he told her taking his hand off of hers.

"No please, you didn't do anything wrong. I guess I'm a little jumpy now and unable to control my actions. I apologize for my rudeness."

"Rudeness?" he said questioningly. "There was no rudeness just a woman struggling to get through an act so ugly no one should ever have to go through it. It's natural for you to want to draw away or flinch or even run. Hell if I had been in your situation I probably wouldn't have let you touch me" he told her gently.

She couldn't help but think of how such a big man could be so gentle. If this had just been a different time and a different place she may have entertained the idea . . . No she told herself. You can't do this or think like this. As she silently chided herself Lily came in and told her the sheriff's deputy was here to see her.

"Good" said Tom, "let's go chat with this fella about what's going on."

He extended his hand as he stood to help Kelly to her feet and then helped her to the kitchen. It wasn't the same deputy as before she noticed, this one was a little shorter and older than the one who came before.

"Dave" Tom said, "it's good to see you. How's the wife and kids?"

"Hi Tom, they're good. I didn't know that you were friends with the complainant."

"The complainant?" Kelly asked.

"Yes ma'am" replied the deputy. "You're the one that is making a complaint. He extended his hand toward her and said "my name is Deputy Kruntz. I'm here to get your statement and find out what happened."

Kelly reluctantly accepted his hand and told him her name. Tom stepped up and interjected between them. "Dave, this is Kelly Price, her husband beat her severely the other night and now she has been receiving prank phone calls. I believe it's the husband, but we don't have any solid evidence of that yet. I told her to phone this in and make a documented report in case something serious arises out of this."

"I'll be glad to. Mrs. Price do you mind going over all of this again with me in your own words?"

"No, not at all" her voice sounded tired and she looked so haggard. The deputy thought to himself that he'd kill the man that ever did this to his wife. What this woman has gone through is just unfathomable.

Kelly explained everything she had been through for the past couple of days beginning with the ordeal she went through with Eric and ending with the last prank call. "So you see it sounded like him but I'm just not sure. I feel as though I'm losing my mind and I have to keep it together for the sake of my children."

Deputy Krantz wrote down everything he needed and called in his report so he could give Kelly a case number. He wrote it down on the back of a business card and handed it to her telling her that she could reach him at the number on the front of the card and if he wasn't in then they could leave him a message and he would retrieve it when he got in.

Kelly thanked him for his time thinking all the while that she was growing a small collection of these things. Tom said goodbye to his friend and walked him to his patrol car.

"Do you really think it's a good idea for you to become involved in this woman's life or personal business?" Dave asked Tom.

"Who else does she have? I'm not dating her" but Dave cut him off.

"You would like to though. I can see it written all over your face. It's your life friend but I'm telling you that I don't believe it's a good idea."

"I don't recall asking you friend" Tom said with some humor "and besides, I'm not dating her yet . . . but I am going to be certain that this son of a bitch doesn't lay another hand on her. She can't be left to her own defenses Dave, she would never make it."

"I understand Tom but just make sure you're careful. I've got to go, they just called in for someone to serve that warrant on her husband. Hopefully we catch that bastard at home."

"I hope so Dave. Will you let me know if you do?"

"Yours will be my first call" he said while getting in his cruiser.

Tom closed the door behind his friend and turned to walk back to Kelly's house. He needed to be sure that she was ok. When he walked back inside her girls were sitting at the table eating ice cream sundaes. They all looked up at him at once.

"Hi girls, I'm Trooper Tom Fielder."

"I know who you are" said Lily, "you were in the living room talking to our mom. Is she going to be ok? Is there something wrong that she's not telling us?"

"No. not at all" he didn't want to frighten four young girls. "I just stopped by to check on your mom and to make sure she had all the pertinent information she needs. She's been through a rough ordeal."

"Yes she has" said Rhonda, "but I think you have a soft spot for her." Tom's eyes widened and his face became slightly flushed. This girl was a little intuitive. "I'm glad you do, because right now she needs someone that can stand up to Eric."

"You call your dad by his first name?" Tom asked.

"He's not my dad" Rhonda said a little heatedly, "he's my step dad. I wouldn't want that asshole for a dad" she told him pointedly.

"I can see he's neither your or my favorite person."

"He's none of our favorite person anymore" Star chimed in "did I say that right?"

They all laughed and said yes. "Will you keep our mom safe?" Star asked, "I don't want my daddy to hurt her anymore. He's never been very nice to her but now he's really mean."

"I'm going to do my best. So tell me, what are your names? Beginning with you" he said to Star.

"My name is Star and that is my oldest sister Rhonda and the one with the blue shirt is Lily and the other one is Sarah."

"I'm very pleased to meet all of you beautiful ladies. You all take after your mother" he told them, with that Rita, Ryan and Kelly walked into the kitchen. "Well if it isn't the lady of the hour" he said smiling.

"Can we get you anything mommy?" asked Star.

"I have everything I need right here in this kitchen" she told them. "I have my beautiful girls, my two best friends and my hero I can't think of anything else I could possibly need."

"I can" said Tom, "a dog."

"Oh mommy could we? Huh mom? Could we get a dog?"

"Now see what you started Mr. Hero?" Rita said smiling.

"They won't let this one go Kell, so you might as well cave now with dignity" Ryan laughed.

"You're right" Kelly said trying not to laugh because it hurt so much "I know when I'm outnumbered. I guess we better start looking for a dog. So, what kind of dog do we get Tom?"

"You need a dog that is going to bark when people come onto your property or to the door. One that will alert you to anyone coming around. But not a puppy, you need a dog that is at least a year old and housebroken."

"Why housebroken?" asked Star.

"Why not a puppy?" asked Lily.

"Do you want him using the bathroom on your floor?" Tom asked with a laugh. "You need a dog that will be indoors with you. You also need one that is old enough to discern between friend and foe and a puppy can't do that. They love everyone equally" he answered smiling. Do you understand why?"

"I understand" Kelly answered. "Well I guess we're going dog shopping."

"I can go online right now" Rhonda said excitedly.

"Ok, but look at the pound first. They have so many homeless animals let's see if we can't save the one we are expecting to save me."

"That's a good idea" everyone chimed at once and Rhonda ran back to her room with Lily, Sarah and Star in tow.

"That was a great idea Tom" Ryan told him. "If absolutely nothing else comes of that dog, those girls will be the happiest on earth."

"They deserve it, they all deserve it, but you have to remember that you need a dog that barks. Well I had better be going. I'm going to take a look around outside. Ryan do you mind showing me around so I can get familiar with the surroundings?"

"Not at all" Ryan said retrieving a light jacket from the coat closet. "Follow me" and the two men headed out the door. Thirty minutes later Ryan returned to the kitchen alone.

"Where's Tom?" asked Rita.

"He left. He said to tell you all goodnight and not to forget about the dog." They all laughed for a minute and Kelly told her friends goodnight.

Then almost as an afterthought she added "I didn't see any headlights leaving the driveway."

"You must not have been watching out of the window" Ryan told her smiling.

"I probably wasn't" she said. "Goodnight guys."

"Goodnight Kell" they said in unison as they watched Kelly walk slowly down the hall.

She stopped at Rhonda's room and told her girls she was going to take her medicine and go to bed then she hugged and kissed them all goodnight and walked back to her room.

Once inside, Kelly removed her clothes and put on her button front night shirt. She pulled the covers down on the bed, opened her bottle of painkillers and took one out. Then she got a bottle of water from her mini fridge and took her pill. She felt as though she were going to break as she laid her body down on the bed and her head on the pillow. With the covers pulled up to her neck, Kelly retrieved her remote off the other pillow and turned on her tv. It was time to watch an old rerun of Murder She Wrote. My how she loved that show, and half way through it her pill kicked in and Kelly was asleep.

CHAPTER SEVENTEEN

Kelly awoke stiff from her slumber reminding herself that she wanted to buy a hot tub. Her thoughts quickly turned to the dog she was supposed to get and thought the sooner the better. Rhonda had slipped a note under her door informing her that she bookmarked some dogs on the computer in her room. Kelly smiled.

Having gotten herself dressed in a short sleeved pull on dress, Kelly headed out to the kitchen. She found a note from Ryan saying he had to go back to work and that Rita was there to help her. Kelly smiled to herself and put the note in her pocket.

Rita came walking out of the living room with a glass of orange juice telling her that the kids had all gone to school. "I hadn't realized I slept so late. I thought it was early" Kelly said looking puzzled.

"It's nine a.m. Kell."

"It can't be, my bedroom clock says it's six-thirty."

"Maybe you need some new batteries for your clock."

"Maybe" she said "but I'm not taking a whole pill tonight, it will be a quarter or a half and that's it."

"You probably just needed the sleep Kell, after all you have been through a lot and you are under a lot of stress."

"I guess you're right Rita but still, I have never missed a day of helping the girls get ready for school or walk them out to the bus."

"They understand perfectly well. Now let's change the subject what is first on our agenda today?"

"I want to go look at the dogs that Rhonda bookmarked or at least some of them. I'm going to grab some coffee and see what she saved."

"Let me grab a cup too and I'll look at them with you."

"Thank you Rita, I really mean it, I don't know what the girls or myself would have done without you or Ryan. You have been my lifesaver."

"Ooooh . . . what flavor?" she asked jokingly.

"Cherry" laughed Kelly, "but in all seriousness, you really have. Now that we have coffee in hand, let's go look at the dogs."

The two of them walked down the hall and into Rhonda's room. Rhonda had left the computer turned on and instructions on how to look at the bookmarks. They clicked on each one and Kelly stopped at the fourth. It was a red and white border collie mix. It was a spayed female that was approximately three years old and was brought in to the pound after her elderly owner passed away. The notes said that she was housebroken and had been a good watchdog.

"That's the one I want to go see Rita and she's only a few miles away."

"You got it. Let me go brush my teeth and get my purse and I'll be ready to hit the road."

"I think I'll try to brush my teeth too" Kelly told her and they both left the room headed in different directions.

Rita drove Kelly to the local pound and they went inside. As they closed the door behind themselves, they were greeted by a cheerful woman sitting behind the counter. "Hello, I'm Becky Keeton welcome to our humble animal abode" she said jokingly as she waved her arm to show the front room. "What can I do for you today?" she asked enthusiastically. She did not seem to pay any particular attention to Kelly's face.

"Hi, I'm Kelly Price and this is my best friend Rita. I was wondering if we could see the border collie mix dog? That is if she is still available."

"She is still available" Becky replied smiling "but I will need you sign in to the visitors log before going back to view the dogs." She picked up a clipboard from the counter and placed it in front of Kelly so she could sign in.

Kelly signed her name and the information it asked for and then handed the clipboard to Rita to do the same. When Rita was finished signing in she handed the clipboard back to Becky who then placed it back on the counter in its original spot.

"Good" said Becky as she got to her feet "now that that is done, if you follow me through these doors I'll show you to the dog you inquired about." Her face wore a bright smile and the woman looked genuinely happy about her work.

They passed through the double doors into a small hallway with several barking dogs in kennels on either side and made a left turn down another hallway. This hallway had even more kennels and a lot more barking dogs, all of which seemed to be saying 'pick me, pick me' Kelly thought to herself. About halfway down the aisle Becky stopped in front of a kennel on her left.

"This is her, the dog you inquired about."

She was a very pretty dog with a medium sized build and rusty red colored fur with a white blaze and a white ruff around her neck that went down her chest and front legs. Her hind legs were both white and she had a white tip on her tail. She was wagging her tail hard and sat down in front of Kelly and began licking her fingers between the chain link openings.

"She's so sweet" Kelly said as she patted the dog through the chain links.

"Yes she is. It's a shame that she had been brought here. You would think that the lady's family would have wanted to keep her but they turned her over to us about three weeks ago. She is spayed, she has had all of her shots and she gets along well with most other animals. She is housebroken and lets you know when she has to go out. Would you like me to bring her out so you can mingle with her?"

"I would love that" Kelly said enthusiastically.

Becky removed a leash that was hanging from the kennel and opened the door and slipped it on the dog. When she brought her out the door the dog immediately jumped in Kelly's lap, whom was already sitting on the floor waiting to meet the dog.

"She likes you already" Becky remarked.

"I'd say" Rita chimed in. "She acts like she's your long lost friend Kell."

"Yes she does" replied Kelly between kisses from the dog. "But the most important factor that I need in my dog is that it needs to bark. Does she bark?"

"Usually she barks at everyone who comes back here to see her, but she never barked at you. I've really never seen anything like it. Now I must warn you, she doesn't particularly like men as well as she does women but I would assume that's because her owner was a woman."

"Wow! She's perfect! When can I take her home?" the excitement shown in Kelly's eyes.

"I will need you to fill out an application and then we will need to stop by your house and view the property where she is going to stay and where she is going to live. Is your yard fenced?"

"Part of my yard is. I have pastures that are fenced with electric wire and I have chain link in the back yard. Why do you ask?"

"We need to know if the dog will be staying inside or out and if they will be allowed to run or if they will be leash walked. Exercise is important for any dog. I will also need some information concerning your vet."

"I don't have a vet other than my large animal vet but I think he cares for dogs too on his barn calls."

"That will be fine. Otherwise if you aren't familiar with the care of a pet then we will educate you before you take her home. So how about we get this application process started?"

"That will be great. How much is the adoption fee?" Kelly asked.

"It's usually around one hundred and eighty five dollars for females, but this one is already spayed and has had her shots so her fee is only one hundred" Becky said smiling.

"How long do I have to wait before I can pick her up?"

"We will have to check your references and like I said we need to make a home visit but it should not take more than a few days to a week."

"Really" Kelly said unable to hide the disappointment in her voice. "It takes that long?"

"Usually, I'm sorry but we have to be certain that these animals are going to good homes and aren't going to end up back here or in a similar situation that brought them here in the first place."

"I understand but I was really hoping that I could take her home today."

"How about I schedule someone to come out to your house today? Maybe myself, and I will do my best to check your references today."

"That sounds wonderful to me" the excitement returning to Kelly's face. "Let's get this application filled out."

Becky returned the dog to her kennel and the three of them went back to the front room. Becky walked over to a filing cabinet and retrieved an application for Kelly. She handed the paperwork to her and Kelly began filling it out. When she had finished, Kelly handed the application back to Becky and told her she was looking forward to her visit.

"Would you like to look at some of the other dogs and give a second and third choice?"

"No. This is the only dog I'm interested in" Kelly told her smiling. "I feel like we have already bonded."

Rita and Kelly told the woman goodbye and walked out to the parking lot to the car. Once inside the car Rita told Kelly that she thought she made a good decision and that she didn't like how long they may have to wait for the dog. She also complained about the high adoption fee and remarked that more dogs would probably get adopted if the fees were lower and the waiting period shorter.

Kelly agreed with her but was excited to know that in a few days she may have one part of the solution to her problem solved.

"Hey mom" Rhonda said as she took off her backpack. "Did you get the dog?" You could see the enthusiasm written all over her face.

"Yes I did as a matter of fact" she told her smiling as best she could. "We just have to wait for our adoption approval."

"Adoption approval?" Sarah said questioningly. "Why? The dog needs a home, we need a dog and they need people to adopt. I don't think it could be any simpler than that" she said as she took her homework out of her backpack.

"They can't let the animals they have go to just any home, so you have to have a home inspection and references checked before they will approve you to adopt. They need to be sure that you will be able to properly care for the animal you adopt and that it won't end up in the same situation that placed it in the shelter to start with."

"Wow!" exclaimed Rhonda, "I didn't know you had to go through all of that or I would have suggested one from the newspaper."

"Now don't be like that" Kelly told her, "they really have to look out for the welfare of the dog. It will all be worth it in the end. She should be placed with us in a few days."

"Well that's a relief, at least we will have a dog to bark if someone comes around uninvited and we'll finally have a family pet." They all laughed together as the girls sat down at the kitchen table to do their homework.

"At least they have already been to the house and inspected inside and out."

"Really? That fast?" Rhonda and Sarah said in unison.

"Yes" Rita said smiling. They told your mom they would come out today and they actually did. Now they only have to do the reference check with your vet and your mom's friends plus they need to be sure of her financial situation."

"Which they could see from my tax return that that is not a problem."

"Your tax return mom? Why do they need that?" asked Sarah.

"To check my finances. They need to make sure that all adoptees are financially able to take care of all of a pet's needs, not just food, water and shelter. My tax returns are all in order and although I'm not able to work right now, we have enough money in the bank to keep us going the rest of the year, including the dog" she laughed.

"That's great to hear" Rhonda told her. "I can't wait to see her."

"Well, as part of the adoption process I have to bring all of you in to meet her anyway before they will release her to me. So guess where we will be going later this afternoon after your sisters get off the bus?"

"To meet the dog?" Sarah asked excitedly.

"You guessed it" said Aunt Rita.

"That is great! I'm going to finish my homework as soon as I can and take a shower" Rhonda told her.

"Save the shower for when we get back home" her Aunt Rita laughed. "The dog hasn't had a bath recently and she is shedding a little."

"Well then, I guess I'll just go like I am" she laughed.

"I'm finished my homework" stated Sarah. "I'm ready to go the minute they get here."

"We don't have too long to wait, and I think I'll let them do their homework when we get home from the shelter." Kelly seemed to be even more excited than her girls. She couldn't wait to go back and see the dog again, she loved her already.

When Lily and Star got off the bus, Kelly, Rita and Rhonda were waiting for them in Ryan's truck. Kelly rolled down the window and told the girls to jump in they were going to meet the dog. The girls squealed with excitement and climbed in the back seat. In just a short period they were at the animal shelter or the local pound as they called it.

Becky was waiting for them at the front counter and smiled as they all walked in. "Are you ready to meet your newest family member?" she asked the girls.

"Yes" said Lily, "you bet" said Sarah "I most certainly am" cried Rhonda "show me the way" said Star all at the same time. They were all grinning from ear to ear.

"Wow" Becky laughed, "I think you are all excited" and she laughed deeply. "Just follow me through these doors" and they all ran along behind her.

They followed Becky through the doors and down the hallway to the second hall and to the kennel. Becky opened the kennel door, put a leash on the little border collie mix and brought her out to meet her potential new family.

The girls cooed at her and petted her and hugged her and all the while the little dog licked their faces and wagged her tail. She never jumped up and she never tried to growl or bark, she just acted like they were her family and she was glad to see them.

"She's perfect" Rhonda told her mother.

"Yes she is" said Sarah.

"Look mom, she loves us already" said Star.

"She loves me the most" laughed Lily while she got her face washed.

When the dog spied Kelly she ran to her and sat at her feet wagging her tail and rubbing her head on Kelly's leg. "I love you too" Kelly told the dog as she scratched her behind the ears.

"I think this settles the matter! I think you have yourselves a dog" Becky told them. "I only have to wait for your vet to return my phone call and you can pick her up after I speak with him. How does that sound?" she asked them smiling.

"Great!" they all said in unison.

"Well, let me put her away so we get the animals fed and close up for the night."

"Thank you for waiting for us" Kelly told her.

"It was my pleasure. I'm just glad that she will be going to such a loving home and family."

"What's her name?" asked Star.

"Daisy" Becky told her, "but you can name her anything you would like."

"How long has she had that name?" Star asked with concern.

"Well, she is three years old, so I would assume three years but I don't honestly know. The family told us her name was Daisy and the dog belonged to one of their family members that had passed away and none of them could keep the dog."

"How sad" said Star "that they would do that to her. After all, she just went through a tragedy too."

"I couldn't agree with you more. You are a very wise young lady and that is one very lucky dog."

"No, we're the lucky ones" Star said and they all agreed.

"Thank you again for letting the girls meet Daisy today" Kelly told Becky.

"You are so very welcome. I'm glad that you liked her, you will be getting a wonderful dog."

"Does everyone have their homework finished?" Kelly asked the girls.

"Yes" they told her.

"Good, let's have a movie in my room. I'm sore and tired and would like to relax with a movie and I would like you guys to join me."

"That will be great" Star said. "How about I make us some popcorn and make you some ice cream?"

"That would be fabulous" Kelly told her. "I'm just going to get a shower and wash my hair. How about you girls take your showers too?" she asked

"Sarah and I already got ours, but Lily and Star haven't had theirs yet."

"I'm first" cried Lily running toward the hall bath. "You always take too long Star."

"That's ok, I don't care" Star called in Lily's direction.

"You can use our shower Star" Rhonda told her.

"Thank you Rhonda" and Star padded happily toward the bathroom that adjoined Sarah and Rhonda's rooms.

CHAPTER EIGHTEEN

Everyone was settled in Kelly's bed ready to watch the movie except Rita and Ryan which were sitting on the love seat on the window side of the room. Star had popped two bags of popcorn and gave her mother three scoops of vanilla ice cream with caramel and whipped cream on top.

Rhonda passed a blanket over to Rita and Ryan since everyone was in their pajamas and the air was slightly chilly in her mother's room. They were all snuggling under covers watching The Hills Have Eyes when the phone rang and made everyone jump. They all laughed while Kelly answered the phone over their little fright and Rita paused the movie so no one would miss any of it.

Kelly's face was drained of color beneath the bruising. All eyes were on her as she said in a low whisper "who is this? What do you want?"

"You know who it is you ungrateful bitch" he screamed. "You no good psycho bitch! How dare you call the cops on me, I'll kill you bitch!"

Even though the voice was distorted Kelly knew it was Eric. The horrified look on her face had Ryan off the loveseat and by Kelly's side in a matter of seconds. "What is it Kelly?" he asked taking the receiver from her hand.

"It's Eric," she whispered, "I know that it's Eric." Kelly's eyes were once again brimming with tears. The fear showed clearly on her face, despite her best efforts to mask it.

Ryan put the receiver up to his ear and walked quickly out of Kelly room so the girls would not hear him. "Look you demented bastard, leave Kelly the hell alone. Haven't you done enough to her? Well you son of a bitch? Answer me! Answer me I said or can you only pick on defenseless women?" Ryan's tone was acidic and seething with venomous anger, but his words fell on dead air. Whoever was on the other end had already hung up.

Kelly was standing directly behind Ryan when he turned around. "What happened Ryan? Is he going to stop?" Kelly's voice was full of panic she was trying to cover.

"I'm so sorry Kell" he said his eyes looking at the ceiling as he drew in a deep breath. "The simple son of a bitch had already hung up on me. I don't think he heard anything I said." He saw the devastated look on Kelly's face as he looked down at her. His stomach tightened as he tried his best to hide his anger and regain his composure.

"That's what he has been doing. When someone else gets the phone he hangs up on them. He only speaks to me and he distorts his voice. I know it's him, it has to be him. Oh geez Ryan I think I'm going nuts."

Ryan put his arms around Kelly's shoulders and felt her flinch. He knew she was trying her best not to be afraid of him but it was just one more reason for him to hate Eric with a passion. He stepped back from Kelly and dropped his arms to his sides telling her was sorry.

"Don't be Ryan. I won't always be this way. You and Rita are my best friends and I don't know what I would do without you. It's just all of this mess. I can't feel comfortable anywhere or with anyone and that sucks because Tom is so nice and I really like him. But somehow I feel like I can't trust anyone that's a man. How do I get over this Ryan? Please tell me what to do before my entire life is destroyed." The tears were falling freely from Kelly's eyes now and Ryan handed her a handkerchief from his pocket.

"Don't worry" he said with a cocky grin, "it's clean. Kelly, you can't let that asshole get to you. He is trying to keep you afraid and he's succeeding."

"I don't know how to not let him get to me. You weren't there that night Ryan you don't know what he did to me. I will never be the same woman as I was before that night. I will never feel safe again especially with these phone calls. It is like a constant reminder that I am worthless."

"Don't you ever say that about yourself again" he said softly. "You are a strong, beautiful, intelligent woman. Don't let him do this to you."

"I just don't see what you see anymore. I am in constant fear. Maybe I should have gone back to him then none of this would have happened."

"That's nonsense and you know it Kelly. It's fear talking right now. You know perfectly well that if you had gone back to him he would have done this sooner or later. The man was a ticking time bomb and he still is only it may have ended up being one of your kids that he took his jealousy and insecurities out on."

"I know you're right Ryan, but I just keep trying to play different scenarios in my head that will help me come up with a better ending."

"Well there is no scenario that will change the ending to what has already happened. It would have had the same outcome no matter what you did. Now let's get back to the movie before the girls start to worry more than they probably already are."

"Ok" she said simply and turned back toward her room walking down the hallway with Ryan by her side.

"Is everything alright?" Rita asked as they walked in, her voice filled with the concern that was in everyone's eyes.

"Yes" Kelly said simply. "Now, how about that movie?"

"Are you sure you really want to watch this one mom? It is really scary" Rhonda asked her with concern.

"This movie is fine" Kelly said laughing lightly, "besides. It's not about my life." Everyone laughed at that answer.

"Thank goodness" Star chimed in "I don't think I could handle knowing there were cannibals living in our woods." That said, everyone broke out into deep laughter and Rita hit the play button on the remote so the movie could resume.

After the movie ended Kelly gave her girls a kiss and hug goodnight and decided that she needed another soak in the bathtub for her aching body. She walked out to the kitchen with Rita and Ryan, opened the cabinet and retrieved a wine glass. She then crossed over to the refrigerator and grabbed out a bottle from the white zinfandel four-pack.

"Would either of you like to share this with me?" she asked looking back and forth from Rita to Ryan to Rita again.

"I will" Rita said reaching in the cabinet for a glass.

"You shouldn't drink that when you're taking pain pills Kell" Ryan told her with concern.

"I'm not. I'm not going to take the pain medicine tonight, it makes me too dizzy. Besides, I feel like a glass of wine to calm my nerves and help me relax a little.'

"You do what you need to do" Rita told her as she opened the small bottle for her and began pouring it equally into both glasses. "Half a glass of wine isn't going to hurt you and if you prefer this over the pain meds then I think you deserve to have it."

"Thank you Rita" she said quietly.

"I didn't mean that you don't deserve a glass of wine honey, I meant that it's dangerous to mix the wine with any kind of prescription drugs."

"I know" she said trying to smile. "I just feel like the wine as opposed to the pills."

"Did you log that call?" Ryan's face was expressionless.

"No, I forgot. I'll do that right now. Thanks for reminding me."

"No problem. Did you call that trooper and let him know it happened again?"

"Not yet, I thought that I would wait a while. I wanted to take a long soak in a hot bath to make my body feel a little less achy" she said trying to smile through stitched lips.

"Well, I think you should and the sooner the better. I mean the sooner you let him know, the fresher it is in your mind."

"Ryan's right Kell, I think you should call Tom and let him know what's happened."

"Ok you two" she said allowing a small giggle to escape "I'll call him as soon as I get back to my room. She put her glass up to her mouth and was having a difficult time trying to drink.

"Here" Ryan said smiling and handing her a straw "use this. I think you'll get more in your mouth." The sound of the laughter emitting from the room sounded good to her. This house felt like a prison lately.

Kelly thanked him for the straw and headed back to her room. Once inside she went into her bathroom and drew a hot bath. When the tub looked like it was deep enough for her to soak her back, she removed her robe and pajamas. Remembering that she was supposed to call Tom and inform him of the call she put her robe back on, took another sip from the straw in her glass of wine and walked back into her room to get the phone.

She looked back on the caller ID and logged the time that the blocked call came through and what was said. She then carried the phone with her into the bathroom and scrolled back on the caller ID to Tom's number and hit send. She dropped her robe, grabbed her glass and stepped into the tub.

She eased herself in to the tepid water, careful not to let the phone get wet or to drop her glass. After about four rings it went to voicemail. "Hi Tom, this is Kelly. I just called to let you know that I received another call tonight and even though the voice was distorted, I'm positive it was Eric. I logged the call but I didn't call the sheriff's office. Well, I hope you have an uneventful night, talk to you later. Bye." Kelly pressed end and placed the phone on the floor beside the bathtub so it wouldn't get wet and lowered herself a little deeper into the tub.

It took all she had not to scream, but the hot water really felt good on her aching body, although her chest and shoulder wouldn't exactly agree. She tried to let the water cover her right shoulder. It was already making her back feel better, or was it the wine? It didn't matter, what mattered was she wasn't going to be under the influence of pain medicine tonight and tomorrow she would be able to get up with her girls.

She laid back against the bathtub pillow that was suctioned to the back of the tub and settled back on it. The water just felt so good. Kelly closed her eyes and let her mind drift to the pretty little dog she saw earlier today that would soon be theirs. She was so excited and relaxed at the same time. She told herself that everything would be better soon. She was about to take another sip of the wine still in her hand when the phone began ringing.

She answered it on the third ring after finding a safe place to put her glass. "Hello" she said with a smile after looking at the caller ID.

"Hello to you" Tom said laughing into the receiver. "I didn't wake you did I?"

"No not at all. I was just soaking this aching body in a hot tub and drinking a glass of wine" she said with a hint of laughter in her voice.

"I always seem to be catching you naked in the tub. Oh I'm sorry, I shouldn't have said that" he sounded regretful.

"You're fine" she said smiling to herself and feeling the blush on her cheeks. "It does seem that every time we talk on the phone I'm in the tub."

"So what happened with this phone call?" he asked.

Kelly went over the entire conversation she had with her caller and let him know that she had already logged the call.

"I'm glad to hear that. He sounds like he's getting braver with his conversation. I'm on duty right now and I will be until eleven. Would you like me to look around when I get off duty? To make sure nothing is amiss?"

"No, there's no need for you to do that. I'll be in bed and you should go home and get some sleep. There's no need to constantly worry over me."

"Well, I do worry about you. There is a psychotic ass harassing you by phone and nothing any one can do about it until you are certain of who the caller is."

"I'm pretty sure that it's Eric. He acts like him and calls me the names that he calls me. His favorite name for me is psycho bitch" she said with sadness in her voice.

The sound of her sadness killed Tom. How could anyone do this to someone like her? She seems to be such a sweet person and so kind. "Unfortunately, that's not enough. You have to be a hundred percent sure. I really want that jerk locked up behind bars" the anger was escaping in his voice. "He really ticks me off."

"Me too" she replied with a giggle. "I'm glad I'm not the only one that feels this way."

"Believe me, you aren't." Tom's radio was going off in the background and he told her he just received a call and had to go. "I'll drop by and check on you tomorrow. Goodnight." With that, he was gone. There was nothing left but silence on the phone.

Kelly couldn't hide the disappointment from herself. She didn't understand why his calls meant so much to her, but they did. He was starting to weigh heavy on her mind. 'Could I really be having feelings for this man?' she asked herself. 'How can that possibly be when I am so afraid to be alone with a man or touched by a man, even Ryan?' But still the thought of Tom thrilled her somehow and she didn't know what to do about that.

Kelly climbed slowly out of the tub and gently dried herself off. She reached for her pajamas and pulled the pants on and then the button front top. She emptied what was left of the wine in her glass in the sink and rinsed them both. Then she picked up the phone and placed it on the charger next to her bed on the nightstand. Pulling back the covers she thought to herself how nice it would be if she just had someone that could hold her and tell her everything was going to be ok? But how can you do that when you're afraid of the entire male species. Of course how can you be afraid of the male species and want one of them so desperately? This was one question with no easy answer.

She lied down in the bed and pulled the covers up to her chest then closed her eyes and waited for sleep to envelop her. But sleep was eluding her.

Sometime during the early hours of the morning sleep laid its claim on Kelly. She was actually in a rather restful sleep when something had awoken her. She couldn't quite put her finger on it. She looked at the phone and picked up from its charger. She scrolled back on the caller ID to see if someone had possibly called and that's what woke her, but the last call had come at nine thirty and that had been Tom.

Then she heard it again. It was a tap on her window. 'Tom said that he wanted to stop by and take a look around, maybe that's him" she thought to herself. Kelly pushed off the covers and eased her aching body out of her warm bed. The satin sheets had slid easily back. Kelly walked over to her window and peered into the darkness outside. She cupped her left hand beside her face on the glass to try to get a better view of what was out there.

She couldn't see anything in the pitch black of night. There weren't even any stars out tonight to cast a little light. She turned away from the window and she heard it again and just about jumped out of her skin. It was a stronger tap on her window. If there had been a tree near there, she would have blamed it on the wind and a branch, but there were no trees near there.

Kelly walked into the bathroom to retrieve her robe and put it on then walked back to the window picking up her flashlight along the way. When she reached the window, she turned on the flashlight and shined the beam of light through it. She still could not see anything. She turned out the light and straightened herself when all of a sudden there was a loud bang on the window. Kelly openly screamed! She knew she saw a hand on her window.

Rita came running into Kelly's room with Rhonda on her heels. "What's wrong Kelly? I heard you scream and you're shaking like a leaf" Rita said as she approached Kelly.

"What happened mom? You sounded like someone was in here with you."

"Not in here" she cried, "my window. Someone was at my window." There was terror in Kelly's voice.

"Great!" exclaimed Rita exasperated. "Of all the nights for Ryan to be called in to work for an emergency, it's while this psychotic ass is still on the loose."

"Was it Eric mom?" fear was taking hold of Rhonda's voice.

"I don't know" Kelly told her, "but I'm not waiting for him to break in. I'm going outside and see what the hell he wants."

"Are you out of your mind?" asked Rita.

"Have you lost your marbles mom? If that psycho is out there he might kill you."

"No, I think he wants to scare me."

"I think he's doing a good job of it, don't you? I can see the fear in your eyes. Don't you dare go out there, call the damn police and let them do their job. You don't need to do it for them."

"Ok you win Rhonda" Kelly said shakily. "Call 911 and report a prowler."

Rhonda grabbed the phone and made the call as her mother instructed. She told the operator that answered what happened and gave them the address. The person on the other end assured her that they would send someone out immediately. Less than ten minutes later a sheriff's deputy pulled in the driveway with his lights flashing.

He came up to the door and asked if everyone was okay and then asked if the intruder had gotten in the house. Kelly explained that he was tapping at her bedroom window and she saw his hand on the pane. He told her he would have tried to get fingerprints, but it was raining and he wouldn't be able to lift any if he tried.

The deputy turned on a bright flashlight and began walking around the yard. Fifteen minutes later he came back and knocked on the door. I didn't see anyone or anything ma'am, but I would advise that you log this incident on your calendar or whatever you are using to log everything on. I am going to give you a case number. I am familiar with what's been going on we have a record of it. You have had to call a few times in the past couple of days.

"I'm sorry" was all that Kelly could manage to get out.

"Don't be ma'am, that's what we're here for. Just please lock up after I leave. Is there anyone you can call to come stay with you ladies?" he asked gently, he could not get the images out of his mind of Kelly's horrific bruises.

"I know someone, but I really don't want to wake him" she said shakily.

"Ma'am, in my opinion it's better to wake him and have a little help than to leave him sleep and have none when you need it. But that's just my opinion."

Kelly looked the young deputy in the eyes and told him she would call her friend right now. "Maybe he won't mind sleeping on the couch" she said shyly with a partial embarrassed smile.

"Good. I've written a complaint number on the back of my card for you just in case you have any further problems" he told her handing her his card. "Call your friend and try to have a good night. If you have any more problems, please don't hesitate to call."

"I will thank you. Thank you for coming out here for me."

"You're welcome ma'am. You ladies try to take it easy and get some rest" and he turned and walked out of the door closing it behind him.

"Are you going to call Mr. Hero mom?" Rhonda asked teasingly. "In all seriousness, I really think you should."

"Yes" Kelly said shaking her head from side to side and smiling. "Hopefully, he isn't sleeping."

Tom answered on the second ring. "Is everything alright?" his voice sounded alarmed.

"I think so" Kelly answered. "I had a small problem just a few minutes ago and the deputy suggested I call a friend to come and stay with us for the night. Ryan was called out of town on an emergency."

"What happened?"

"I had someone tapping my bedroom window tonight and he slammed his hand on it to make sure I saw it I think."

"Give me fifteen minutes I need to throw some clothes on."

"Oh no, I woke you up. You were already in bed. No, don't come, it's raining and I don't want you to have to get out of a warm bed to rescue me for something that may be nothing."

"Nonsense, if a deputy told you to call someone to stay with you, then you need someone to be there. I won't take no for an answer and besides, I'm already dressed. I'll be there in ten minutes now" he said laughing "and nothing you can say will keep me away."

Kelly smiled and thanked him then hung up the phone. 'What are you going to do now?' she thought to herself. "Tom will be here in ten minutes" she told Rita and Rhonda. "I can't let him see me in pajamas. What am I going to do? It's way too early to get dressed." She looked genuinely panicked about her clothing situation.

"Mom, why don't you put on one of your nightgowns and your robe? That would work."

"I believe you're right Rhonda, thank you."

"Oh you are just so cute" teased Rita, "you're like a school girl with her first crush coming over to study." They all laughed together and Kelly went back to her room to change.

As soon as she had pulled her robe around her, there was a strong knock on the kitchen door. 'Man, he wasn't kidding about being ten minutes' she said to herself and headed to the kitchen to answer the door, but it wasn't Tom's face peeking through the window.

CHAPTER NINETEEN

Kelly tried to scream, but the sound would not come out. The face staring at her through the window of the kitchen door was pure evil. "Oh no, please no" Kelly cried. The face was distorted pressed against the glass and she realized that she didn't lock the door after the deputy left.

Kelly threw her hands out toward the lock, having difficulty with her right arm. She was trying to turn the lock before her intruder realized it wasn't latched. It was too late and her efforts were to no avail. As Kelly's left hand reached the lock, the door swung open knocking her to the side. She realized that he was wearing a mask to distort his face. It was a mask cut from a pair of pantyhose.

Kelly was trying to stand up and trying hard to find her voice, but it was lost to her. Fear overrode her ability to speak. She felt the strong hand dig in to her left shoulder and pick her up to her feet. "Oh God please don't let any of them get out of bed. Please don't let this monster hurt them too. God please don't let him kill me. Oh God please! She prayed to herself while beginning to sob.

"You bitch" he whispered hoarsely. "You no good bitch! I know what you did and now you're going to pay."

Kelly found a small part of her voice and tried to plea with the man. "P p please don't hurt me" she stammered as he pulled her through the threshold of the kitchen door. "I beg you, please don't hurt me. I'll do whatever you want Eric, I swear I will." Kelly felt a searing pain as he punched her in the back. She felt her breath catch in her lungs and she couldn't draw in or out. She was helpless as her captor drug out of the house.

He picked her up and threw her over his shoulder like a rag doll. Kelly felt as though she were going to die when suddenly she gained the ability to breathe again. She began punching the back of her captor desperately trying to get in a good blow. She slipped further down his back and drove her left hand as hard as she could between his legs as he walked. She must have had a good connection because he dropped her as he stumbled to the ground.

When he hit the ground with his knees, Kelly took advantage of the moment and ran. She ran as fast as her wounded and battered body would allow her to run. Suddenly she felt a sharp, searing, burning pain in her left leg. She stifled her cry and reflexively reached down to her left leg where the pain was emanating.

She could feel an object protruding from her calf and the wet warmth trickling beneath it. She instinctively pulled the object from her calf and realized it was a short bladed knife. She removed the belt from her robe and quickly tied it around her wound to try and stop the bleeding. Out of fear she threw the object away from her and struggled to her feet and began to run as best she could.

She looked behind her but couldn't see much in the pitch dark and rain that was beginning to fall harder. She could hear her intruder coming toward her and began running as best she could away from the direction of the sound. "Oh God, where is Tom? He said ten minutes. Where is he?" she whispered shakily through ragged breaths.

"I can hear you bitch! When I catch up to you I'm going to kill you" the voice behind her was saying. Then raising his voice a few octaves he yelled "Do you hear me bitch? I'm going to kill you!"

Kelly had never felt such fear in her life. She thought that she could never feel fear like she did at the hands of Eric a few nights ago again, but she was wrong. Dead wrong! Kelly ran toward the back of the garage at the end of the driveway just past the house. Now she wished it had been an attached garage so she could get back in the house and then reconsidered that thought. If she could get in the house from there then so could the maniac trying to kill her.

Where could she hide? The pain in her back was searing and the throbbing in her calf was almost unbearable. How would she be able to hide from the madman trying to kill her? Kelly desperately tried to run. She could hear the footsteps coming faster behind her. "I can hear you bitch. Make this easy on yourself and just give up. If you give up now, I'll make this quick and painless."

The tears were streaming uncontrollable down her cheeks. "God please don't let him kill me, but most importantly, please don't let him hurt my kids." Kelly made it behind the garage and cut across the field toward the graveyard. She had to get this man away from her house and the graveyard on the back of the property was the only place she could make it to in her condition.

The rain was making it difficult for her to find solid tread without slipping, but if it were difficult for her to find traction in bare feet, then it had to be more difficult for him in shoes. 'I won't slow down' she thought to herself 'I have to do this.' The rain was stopping and the clouds were moving allowing the moon to shine its light on the ground. "Not now" she said allowed, crying. "I need to make it to the graveyard unseen."

"I can see you bitch" said the terrifying voice. "I'm going to make you suffer for what you've done."

"Where the hell is Tom" she cried aloud.

"Your boyfriend isn't coming to help you. He's been watching you for me."

"You're lying Kelly sobbed, you're lying." Kelly then ran with all her might and made it to the graveyard. In the distance she could see headlights. 'Please let that be Tom' she prayed in her mind. 'Please let him save me.'

"I think you must be running out of steam" said the distorted voice. "It looks as though my backup has arrived" he laughed hysterically. "You are as good as dead bitch and no one can save you from me."

Kelly knelt down behind a tombstone and tried to peak around the side of it. Her heart was pounding, her mind was racing and her leg was beginning to bleed through her tourniquet. Now more than ever she felt as though she were hiding from death. How ironic for her to hide from a madman trying to kill her, in a graveyard behind a tombstone. If this had not been a life or death situation she would have been inclined to laugh about her situation.

Tom got out of his car and walked up to the kitchen door cautiously. Instinctively he pulled out his gun and slowly walked through the threshold. He peered around the counter and looked around the kitchen moving cautiously around the room. He made his way to the living room silently and used his flashlight to see by so as not to turn on any lights giving away his position.

After checking the room thoroughly and checking the two rooms off of it, both closets and the bathroom, he began to move back to the kitchen to look on the other side of the house. He paused in the doorway to the kitchen when he came face to face with Rhonda.

"What are you doing? The deputy had looked around outside and the guy never came in the house, and don't you know how to close a door?" Rhonda asked in exasperation.

"That wasn't me. I didn't leave the kitchen door open it was open when I got here."

"What do you mean? Mom closed the door behind the deputy when he left, I saw her." Rhonda couldn't hide the terror in her voice or the horrified look on her face. There was a sensation of fear taking over her entire being. "Where is my mom?"

"I don't know. I haven't checked her room yet, have you?" he asked her calmly.

"No, no I haven't. Oh please tell me he didn't get my mom." Rhonda was becoming hysterical and Tom needed to get her emotions under control, especially if her sisters woke up.

"Rhonda calm down. I need you to keep it together. I need you to help me look for your mother and I need you to be strong in case your sisters wake up. Where is the last place you saw your mother?"

"Here in the kitchen" she said, tears beginning to choke her voice. "You have to find her, she's my mom she's all we have."

"I will, I will find her. Trust me Rhonda. I need to check the rest of the house and I need you to stay behind me."

"I will" she said quietly trying to hold back her tears.

The two of them began their search, Tom didn't like looking for Kelly with her teenage daughter in tow, but it was better than leaving her in the kitchen alone. He decided that he would have her stay in her room as soon as he checked it out.

He quietly went through Lily's room without waking her, then the hall bath followed by Rita's room. She was lying in bed with a sleep mask on. He then checked Sarah's room and she awoke while he was searching her closet. She was startled to see a strange man searching her room with a gun in his hand.

"Rhonda, stay here with Sarah and don't leave this room. If Star wakes up I'll send her in here with you. I'll tell her to knock twice so you will know who it is."

Rhonda nodded her head in agreement and sat on the bed beside Sarah as Tom disappeared through the door into the hall. As he approached Rhonda's room he had an uneasy feeling. He felt as though he were searching in the wrong direction and that he was needed outside now. 'Why did you stop for coffee?' he chided himself silently. 'If you hadn't stopped this wouldn't have happened. Of course maybe nothing happened. Maybe she's in her room and left the door open for you.'

Tom continued searching the rest of the rooms just in case there was an intruder. Star was sleeping peacefully and never stirred while he searched her room and closet. He couldn't help but look at her angelic face while she slept unaware of what was going on. The last room to search was Kelly's. He entered her room silently and shown his flashlight around while walking through it. He searched both closets and then noticed the pajamas on the floor.

'Why would she take off her pajamas in the middle of the night?' he thought to himself. He walked to her bathroom and shown the light inside. He looked in the shower, around the corner at the commode and in the linen closet. Her linen closet was bigger than his bathroom he laughed to himself. He looked in the bathtub and on the sink counter. He noticed the wine glass on the counter turned upside down to drain.

"Where are you Kelly?" he asked aloud and headed back out of the room and into the dark hall.

Kelly was crying. "I'm going to kill you bitch! You can't hide from me" said the voice laughing hideously. "I'm going to make you suffer you ungrateful psycho bitch."

Kelly couldn't tell if he were getting closer or if he was just talking louder. She just knew that if she didn't get away or hide well enough, she would be killed. Kelly ducked back behind the grave as the clouds recovered the moon and took away the sliver of light. Kelly used that moment to drag herself to the next tombstone.

"I can still hear you bitch! You'll pay for deceiving me."

Unable to control herself she screamed "I knew it was you Eric. You can't disguise your voice from me. Leave me alone, please leave me alone. I'll drop the charges, I'll drop the protective order, I swear I will" she pleaded with him.

"It's too late for that and I'm not Eric you stupid bitch." He began laughing again hysterically, hideously. She could hear him walking closer and wanted to close her eyes like a little girl and pretend that if she couldn't see him he couldn't see her. "I'm getting closer Kelly" he said. "Closer than you think."

"This won't do you any good," she pleaded, not realizing that the more she spoke the better he could follow her voice to find her. "They're going to know who it was, they'll find you" she cried.

"Who Kelly? Who is going to know? It's raining Kelly, even a trickle will wash away any evidence of the crime about to unfold. I'm going to kill you and no one is going to stop me."

Kelly was scared out of her mind. She was praying frantically, begging God not to let her die and to keep her children safe. Then she had a thought. A crazy stupid thought. It would probably get her killed, but it would get her killer caught.

She heard that voice again. That horrible distorted voice and her life saving thought fluttered away. "I'm here Kelly."

Kelly looked all around her terrified. It was beginning to rain again and the pain was becoming excruciating. Her leg was throbbing unmercifully and her back felt like it could break in two. Not to mention her chest that felt like it was being crushed with every breath she took. Her running like a madwoman for her life wasn't helping matters either. This man was going to kill her and she was only prolonging the inevitable. Kelly began to pray frantically. Her tears were burning her eyes. She knew she could no longer run from this man. She knew her hiding place wouldn't protect her much longer. The only thing she had left were her prayers.

Kelly prayed "God please I beg you, please let me get out of this alive. I can't do this alone, I need you. Please help me, send someone to help me, please God please don't let me die." The rain pelted her face and it was becoming even harder to see between the rain and her tears.

"When I find you you're dead bitch. I'm going to enjoy killing you too. I gave you a chance to make this easy on yourself and you refused. It won't be my fault that you die a slow and painful death" and he began to laugh sinisterly.

Kelly thought she saw a shadow and she began to scream hysterically at the top of her lungs. She was certain he was right beside her and she was not going without someone hearing her. As she let out another hysterical scream, she felt the hand grasp the back of her robe and tug hard.

Tom heard the hysterical screams coming from the back of the property. He ran out of the kitchen door leaving it ajar behind him. He had one thing and one thing only on his mind. He had to get to the woman who was taking over his heart. He knew she was in serious trouble and he ran blindly toward the sound of the screams with his revolver in hand. He clicked his flashlight on again and broke out in a dead run.

CHAPTER TWENTY

As the monster behind her pulled her robe viciously, trying to strangle her, Kelly let her left arm fall back the robe fall loose from it. She then twirled immediately so that her right arm could escape the garment being used to entrap her and fled as fast as she could while he fell backward from tugging so hard on an empty garment.

Luckily Kelly knew where the tombstones were in the graveyard, an advantage point her would be assassin didn't have. She heard him swear as he tripped over one of the graves. Kelly could not run fast, the pain had engulfed her from her head to her feet. She was already four headstones away from her tormentor when she heard him yelling at her.

"You bitch! You no good lousy bitch, I'm going to kill you."

With a chest feeling like it were going cave from pain, a back that felt like it was broken in two and a leg that was throbbing and burning Kelly tried to run even farther. But now she had dizziness on top of everything else. Kelly knew she must be losing more blood. She hid behind the grave and tried her best to tighten her makeshift tourniquet. She had to slow the bleeding down or she was afraid she would bleed to death.

She felt strong arms grab her by her shoulders. Her heart was pounding, her adrenaline pumping. She fought and fought hard to free herself from the clutches of the man who was about to kill her. He turned her without effort to face him. The pantyhose mask made him look hideous in the dark with the rain pelting on them. With all her might she swung her knee up and connected solidly with his manhood. He squeezed tighter as he dropped to the ground and Kelly began frantically kicking away at him. She connected with his face and he loosened his grip on her right shoulder.

The moment she felt his grip loosen, Kelly began kicking harder and pulling away. She broke free and he grabbed her by the right ankle as she began to run away. "Oh God please, please let me break free" she prayed aloud as she kicked wickedly at her captor.

"You can't get away from me bitch" he screamed at her back. "I'll kill you, I'm going to kill you" venom was dripping from his words.

"Not on my watch" said a voice in the distance. "Let her go you son of a bitch."

"It's Tom" cried Kelly to no one in particular. "Oh dear God thank you" she said and began frantically kicking at the man holding her ankle with a stronger force. "Let me go" and kicked back with a vengeance. This time it connected with the man's face and he let go grabbing at his face.

Kelly chose that moment to run toward the garage screaming "Tom, Tom."

"I'm right here Kelly" he said reaching out for her as her attacker caught her once more. He had her by the hair and yanked back hard.

"You're mine now" he cried. "Now it's time to pay for what you did" he said venomously.

Tom aimed his gun at the man pulling Kelly backward by the hair. He pointed his flashlight in their direction and Kelly could see the light of the flashlight reflect off the gun for a brief moment.

"Let her go or I'll shoot" Tom commanded. "Don't think for an instant I'm bluffing."

Kelly turned to face the man pulling her by the hair and mustered the energy to kick him with a powerful force in his manhood once more. Her attacker dropped to his knees letting go of Kelly's hair. Tom ran up and pulled Kelly out of the way while he delivered a forceful blow to the man's chest knocking the wind out of him.

Even with the wind knocked out of him, the man reached for Tom's gun and grabbed his arm pulling him to the ground. The two men rolled on the wet ground each with a hand on the weapon. Kelly was watching horrified as the two men fought for control of Tom's gun.

She wanted to hide her eyes as the flashlight beam kept bouncing all around as the two men continued their struggle. Suddenly a shot rang out and the rolling stopped the beam of light shown toward the graveyard. Kelly could see movement and one body rolled as the other seemed to be slowly getting to its feet.

"No, no oh please no" Kelly cried as she watched the man rise to his feet slowly. Her chest was aching, her leg throbbing and her head reeling with dizziness. She began to slowly limp backward because she could no longer put pressure on her leg.

The body was now fully erect and the beam of light was now shining toward her. "Oh God please no, please no" she frantically cried. "Please don't, please don't" she didn't have the strength to even plea for her life properly she thought.

A hand reached out toward her grabbing her left arm. "It's me Kelly. It's Tom. Everything is going to be ok. I shot the son of a bitch while we fighting for the gun. It's over sweetie" he said pulling her in toward him.

"Oh Tom, I thought that was him. I thought he was going to kill me, I thought that he had killed you" she sobbed hysterically.

"I'm okay, but we need to get you to the house and we need to call you ambulance. I think he's going to need a meat wagon" he said pointing with the flashlight toward the motionless body lying on the ground. "Are you alright?" he asked her quietly.

"Yes, I I'm okay" she stammered. "I'm just bleeding a little."

"Where? Where are you bleeding" he asked trying to shine the flashlight toward her face.

"My leg, he stabbed my leg. Well actually he threw a knife at me and it landed in my leg" she cried.

"Where? What part?"

"My left calf" she told him.

Tom shined the flashlight toward her left calf and could see her makeshift tourniquet. "Good job Kelly. We need to get you back to the house, but first I want to handcuff this son of a bitch in case he isn't dead" he told her pointing at the man lying on the ground.

Tom reached behind him and pulled a pair of handcuffs from his back pants pocket and pulling the man's hands behind his back, cuffed him. Then he reached in his jacket pocket and grabbed his cell phone. He quickly dialed 911 and told them where he was and the circumstances of his being there. He told them he needed an ambulance.

Leaving the man lying on the ground, Tom picked Kelly up in his arms and carried her to the house. When they reached the kitchen doorway Kelly asked him who the man was on the ground.

"I don't know. I couldn't see his face, but we will know when they get out here. We'll pull the stocking mask off his face and then we'll be able to identify him.

Once in the kitchen, Tom gently placed Kelly on a chair. "You know we really need to quit meeting like this" he laughed and then he gently kissed her lips. "I'm sorry, did I hurt you?" he asked sincerely.

"No. It was nice. I haven't had a kiss in almost a year" she laughed. "I just never knew this was the way you got them." They both laughed.

Tom walked over to the sink and grabbed a dish towel from the rack and wet it. He then rung it out and walked back over to where Kelly still sat on a chair. He gently removed the sash of the robe and looked at the wound. "That looks pretty deep to me. I'm afraid you're going to need stitches." He quickly tied the sash back around her leg to slow the bleeding.

They could see the lights from the emergency vehicles flashing up the road. Tom patted her knee and said he needed to wake Rita so she could sit with the kids while Kelly went to the hospital. Kelly smiled at him and watched through the doorway as the ambulance and police cars pulled in her driveway. This wasn't going to be fun but at least she had Tom.

"Thank you God for keeping me safe and sending Tom out to find me. Thank you so much! I love you God" Kelly prayed aloud.

Rita came into the kitchen, tears in her eyes. "Oh my goodness Kelly, I can't believe this happened to you and I slept through it all. What kind of friend am I?" she said wiping tears from her cheeks and eyes.

"A good one! Eric is out there, Tom shot him. He won't be bothering me anymore" she said shakily. I was so scared."

The paramedics came in and examined Kelly and her wounds. They told her that the knife wound looked clean and they didn't think it struck an artery. They believed it was bleeding because of all the movement.

They worked on Kelly while Tom went out back with the deputies and another trooper to retrieve the body of the man Tom shot. Kelly was loaded onto the ambulance and assured that Tom would meet her at the hospital shortly. He had to give his statement to the officers at the scene.

When Tom made it to the hospital, Kelly was already stitched up and had gotten a tetanus booster. "Did they get Eric's body out of the yard?" Kelly asked. "I don't want the girls to see it that can be traumatizing" she told him.

"We removed the body Kelly and I need to talk to you about that." He looked haggard. It had to be the events of the night, he had to be exhausted.

"What's wrong Tom?" she asked puzzled. "Please tell me the girls didn't see him" she said shakily.

"No, but we need to talk about the body."

"The body has a name Tom. It's Eric right? It has to be Eric" she almost didn't recognize the sound of her own voice.

"It wasn't Eric. It was Deputy Parsons."

Kelly's mouth dropped and her eyes widened. "Now what do I do?" she asked, "I thought this was over." A new kind of fear was seeping through her veins.

"It is Kelly. We now know why you couldn't recognize the voice" he reassured her, "because it wasn't Eric's. It was Deputy Parsons using a voice modifier."

"But why would he do something like that to me? I didn't know him before yesterday."

"I don't know. Let's just concentrate on this hearing coming up Monday and take it from there." He smiled at her warmly and she let him help her walk out of the hospital after collecting her discharge papers and help her in the car. Monday was just around the corner.

Kelly was up before the kids Monday morning and she made pancakes for breakfast. She had already talked to Tom who was going to be at the hearing today. Kelly was really nervous, but didn't want to let it show. She called the girls to get their breakfast and after they were finished and had collected their backpacks, she kissed them goodbye for school.

Ryan told her that he would be there to put Lily and Star on the bus so she would be able to head out to court since she needed to be there by eight thirty. When she arrived, Mrs. Stanton and Tom were both there waiting for her along with her appointed attorney.

"Mrs. Price, this is Mrs. Gledding. She is the attorney that is going to represent you for your final protective hearing."

"It's nice to meet you" Kelly said while extending her left arm to the attorney. "Please pardon me, but I can't really use my right arm."

"No apologies are necessary Mrs. Price, I understand completely" she said looking sympathetic. "We just need to go over what you said in your order and how much emergency money you are asking for."

"I believe that I asked for five hundred dollars a week" Kelly told her. "Is that too much?"

"No, it's more like it's not enough. Your husband should be giving you at least a thousand a week based on both of your salaries and the fact that you won't be able to work for quite some time."

"I didn't realize I could ask for more" Kelly told her.

"That's why you have me, however, you already stated the amount that you want" Mrs Gledding told her smiling.

"Now, let's walk inside. Trooper Fielder, I'm going to need you wait out here when they call our case."

"No problem" he told her and held the door as the three ladies entered the courtroom.

Eric was already sitting inside. He was sitting with a well-dressed attorney and smiling wickedly at Kelly. The smile was meant to be intimidating and it was, but Kelly wasn't going to let him know that. She took her seat next to her attorney and Mrs. Stanton and Tom took a seat next to her.

She was lost in thought when she heard the bailiff say "All rise, the Honorable Judge Martin C. Jackson presiding."

"Please be seated" he said as he sat in his chair.

The first case called was Price verses Price final protective order. Kelly was extremely nervous and it showed clearly upon her face. The judge looked at her and then despicably at Eric. "Mrs. Price, you are here today to move forward on a final protective order are you not?"

"Yes I am Your Honor."

The attorneys introduced themselves and told the judge who they were representing. Much to Kelly's surprise, the hearing went quickly and smoothly. Eric had denied that he ever struck her but the judge found enough evidence from the hospital reports, Trooper Fielder's testimony, pictures of Kelly's face and body as well as the bruises she still had and the stitches that had not yet been removed from her lip.

He also found that Eric would pay her eight hundred dollars a week in emergency family maintenance money for her and the children since he had the right to modify the amount. He had asked her if she were seeking a divorce and she told him yes. He told her that he hoped she pressed charges and would follow them through. She told him that she had filed and she would follow through.

He went over the names of everyone named in the petition and the schools the children attended. Eric was ordered not to contact any of them in any means or go to their home, work or schools. He was asked if he understood and he said yes.

The bailiff walked Kelly and her attorney out first so she could pick up her paperwork and told her they would hold Eric until she had left the building. Kelly felt complete relief.

"How soon can I file for my divorce?" Kelly asked Mrs. Gledding.

"As soon as you want to" she replied.

"I would like to file today."

"Meet me in my office Thursday at ten a.m. and we will begin the divorce procedures. You have grounds for immediate divorce"

"Thank you" Kelly told her with tears in her eyes.

"You're welcome, I'm glad to be able to help."

The lady at the counter had the protective order ready and Kelly signed for her paperwork with shaky hands. Her hands were shaking so hard that she almost dropped the papers after they were handed to her. She thanked Mrs. Stanton and her attorney once again and agreed to meet her attorney Thursday.

Tom held the door for Kelly as they exited the courthouse and helped her get in his car. He took her for coffee and then back to her house. "How about if I come over tonight?" he asked.

"I would like that" she said nervously.

"Are you okay?"

"I'm fine, just nervous about today."

"Don't be. The worst part is behind you for now. You don't have to worry about anything else until the state makes its case against him. Everything is going to be fine" he said gently caressing her hand.

"I hope you're right" she said smiling.

Tom drove Kelly back to her house and walked her inside. "Do you need me to stay with you for a while?" he asked lightly.

"I would love for you to. Maybe just sit with me until I fall asleep. I feel exhausted" she told him smiling into his eyes.

Those eyes were really getting to him. "Ok then, let's get you ready for a nap" he laughed.

Kelly took Tom's hand in hers and walked back to her bedroom with him. "Are you sure you don't mind sitting with me until I fall asleep?" she asked shyly.

"One hundred percent sure" he told her smiling. "Lead the way" he continued saying and pointing toward the hall.

Kelly walked him back to her bedroom and told him to sit on the bed while she changed. He sat down on the edge of her bed and Kelly went into her bathroom and changed into a long T-shirt and shorts.

Kelly came back out and climbed up on the bed beside Tom. She got up for a moment and pulled her covers down so she could slide in the bed. "Satin sheets huh?" Tom said to her raising one eyebrow.

"Yes, it's the only kind I like" she laughed.

"How did I know you were a high maintenance woman?" he chuckled.

"Lucky guess" she said looking into his eyes. "Now are you going to help me get to sleep?" she asked smiling

"I most certainly am" he said, as he stretched out alongside her, gently rubbing her right arm. "Am I hurting you?" he asked quietly.

"No, it feels good" she said turning to look at him.

"I know how much this arm has been bothering you, I don't want to make it worse" and he leaned in and kissed her gently on her lips. "I can't wait until those lips heal and I can give you a real kiss" he teased.

"Me either" she said yawning.

"I'm going to stay here until you fall asleep and when I leave, I'll lock the door behind me. You did give all of your girls a key to the house didn't you?"

"I most certainly did, just like you told me to" and reaching across her chest with her left arm, she pulled him in tighter against her, so she could feel his warmth next to her. She must have fallen asleep quickly she thought as she was barely able to make out the phone ringing.

"What is wrong with me?" she asked herself aloud and then recognized the noise she was hearing as the phone. She grabbed the receiver and said "Hello, hello?"

"You no good bitch! You betrayed me."

"You're not supposed to call me. Didn't you listen to anything that the judge said?" Kelly asked trying not to let her voice show how afraid she was.

"About as well as you listened to your vows. I'm going to kill you bitch, and no one will be able to stop me" Eric said in a sinister voice.

Kelly dropped the phone on the bed and ran to her bathroom for her robe. Her mind was racing a million thoughts per second. As she came back out of the bedroom her phone began ringing again. Kelly just stared at it unable to move. 'Why is he doing this to me?' she thought to herself. She left the phone go to voicemail as she continued to stare at it and then ran to the kitchen as best her injuries would allow.

When she reached the kitchen, she checked the lock. It was bolted. Tom had flipped the automatic deadbolt when he left. Feeling relief and telling herself it was just a phone call and he would never come to her house after being issued the protective order Kelly got a Coke and a glass of ice and went back to her bedroom to change before the girls got home.

She sat the glass on a coaster on her nightstand and began pulling off her clothes when she heard a noise coming from her bedroom window. She looked up and saw a face pressed against the glass. The face backed off the window pane and smiled evilly. Kelly screamed . . .

Find out more of what happens to Kelly Price
in Theresa Moretimer's next novel . . .

WHEN DEATH COMES STALKING

About The Author

Theresa Moretimer was a victim of domestic violence and went through several years of counseling and awareness programs. Theresa enjoys giving lectures and has made public statements for the governor of her state to help end this tragedy. She is divorced, a mother of four daughters and lives on a small farm in a quiet community. She enjoys writing, singing, cooking, horseback riding, family game nights and movie nights with her children as well as gardening, fishing, camping and ghost hunting.